MW01487900

Awakened Within

A Vienna Rossi
Paranormal Mystery

MICHELLE ANN HOLLSTEIN

Copyright © 2011 Michelle Ann Hollstein
All rights reserved. No part of this book may be reproduced or
transmitted in any form or by any means, electronic or mechanical,
including photocopying, recording, or by any information storage and
retrieval system, without permission in writing from the copyright
owner. This is a work of fiction. Names, characters, places and
incidents either are the product of the author's imagination or are used
fictitiously, and any resemblance to any actual persons, living or dead,
events, or locales is entirely coincidental.

Book Cover Art by: <u>SelfPubBookCovers.com/ violaestrella</u>

Thursday, May 12
Chapter 1

A flash of red... Wobbling, unbalanced... Muffled music... Uncontrollable dizziness... An ear shattering scream that wasn't her own...

With a jolt, Vienna Rossi sat straight up in bed. She ran her fingers into her thick tangled mass of hair. The room was dark and she could hear a chorus of crickets chirping outside her bedroom window. Taking a deep breath, she held it for a moment then exhaled, trying to calm the rapid beating of her heart. This was the third night in a row this week that she awoke because of a nightmare. And not a series of nightly scares, but the same disturbing dream that had been haunting her for the last few weeks. It was becoming more frequent and it wasn't getting any easier to deal with.

Throwing her pillow at the window to quiet the annoying crickets, she plopped back down on her bed and glared at the ceiling. Her eyes were adjusting to the dark and she could almost make out the bumps and molded shapes in the popcorn spray. She turned onto her side and stared at the stacks of canvases of all different sizes leaning against the wall. Some were finished paintings, some were not.

Realizing she wasn't much of a threat, the crickets continued with their chirping. Vienna pressed her pillow over her ear trying to drown them out. She squeezed her eyes shut and hoped to fall back asleep, but there was too much on her mind. The dreaded feeling that the nightmare wasn't going to go away until she did something about it plagued her.

She sighed. She might as well get up. "I'm up already!" she growled at no one in particular. "I get it!"

Scuffling her feet across the wooden floorboards, she stopped at her closet and yanked out a black duffle bag. Snatching a few random tank tops and a couple of T-shirts from the hangers and three pairs of jeans, she began to pack. It didn't matter that she was dead tired. The dream wouldn't let her rest until she solved the problem. She wasn't exactly sure how she knew this. She just did.

***

Settling down in a seat three rows from the front of the plane, Vienna searched her purse for something to take for motion sickness. If she didn't take it now, she knew she'd pay for it later. Popping a little yellow pill into her mouth, and slipping on her trusty pressure point wrist bracelet for traveling, she settled in for the flight.

Vienna dabbed powder on her shiny nose and stared at her bloodshot eyes in the small round mirror of her compact. She sighed while putting on sparkly red lip-gloss. She feared that no amount of makeup could make her look less scary. Frowning she removed her black plastic rimmed glasses and applied dark brown eyeliner along her eyelids.

A little better, she thought, taking in her reflection. She slipped her glasses back on and tossed her makeup into her purse. She was thankful that the two seats on either side of her were empty, giving her some peace and quiet. She wasn't much in the mood for small talk with strangers. Over her shoulder, she looked out the porthole window and watched the sunrise.

The engines roared to life and the pilot's muffled voice droned over the intercom system. Vienna leaned her head back and closed her eyes. She was too tired to try to focus on what he was saying. For a moment or two, her mind drifted into a deep dreamless sleep.

When Vienna opened her eyes, she was quite surprised. She hadn't even realized she'd fallen asleep. And she thanked God that it was a dreamless sleep and not the same reoccurring dream that had been taunting her. Maybe she was being rash by hopping on the first flight out; though at the time she felt compelled to do so.

She wondered how she'd explain this to her father. It was bad enough she charged a last minute plane ticket to his credit card, but she was also skipping out on her college classes in her senior year right before finals. He'd never understand her insatiable need to chase after a nightmare. Hell, she didn't understand it herself. It was just something she had to do. Deep down inside, it just seemed right. No matter how silly.

Vienna turned her head to the side and blinked. There was a man sitting next to her in the seat closest to the aisle, holding up a *Sky Mall* magazine. She had gotten so lost in her thoughts she had not noticed him. He was hard to miss too, because he was so good looking, which made matters worse. Just a few minutes ago, she'd been asleep. She really hoped she hadn't been snoring or even worse, drooling.

"Do people really buy these?" he asked, chuckling, pointing to a talking mug that announced the temperature of your beverage.

Vienna smiled politely and shrugged. She dabbed at the corner of her mouth with the back of her hand in hopes of finding no unwanted drool. To her relief, she found none. "I guess so."

The man appeared to be in his late twenties or early thirties with sandy brown hair, blue eyes, and the most gorgeous smile Vienna had ever seen. Feeling a little flustered, all she could think about now was whether she had brushed her teeth. She'd been in such a hurry this morning, packing her suitcase and catching a last minute flight that she hadn't spent much time on her appearance. At three in the morning, looking beautiful was the last thing on her mind.

The flight attendant pushing the drink cart up the aisle stopped at their seats. Vienna watched her as she poured drinks for the couple sitting in front of her and began to ponder on what she was in the mood for. Something caffeinated was the answer she came up with. The flight attendant rolled the cart forward and stopped.

"A diet Coke, please," Vienna said.

"Would Pepsi be okay?" the flight attendant asked, filling a clear plastic cup with ice.

"Yeah, sure. That's fine," Vienna said. "As long as it's diet." She pulled down the tray attached to the back of the seat in front of her.

"Peanuts?" asked the flight attendant, as she handed Vienna the cup of soda and a small square napkin.

"Yeah, sure," Vienna said, setting her drink in the circular indent on the tray. "Thanks."

The woman handed her a tiny bag of dry roasted peanuts and moved on.

"Not even honey roasted," the man next to Vienna complained, watching her tear open the corner of the bag. "Airlines have gotten so cheap."

"Didn't you want anything?" Vienna asked. She just realized that the flight attendant hadn't even asked him.

"Nah," he said. "Not like I need it." He returned his attention to the *Sky Mall* magazine and chuckled again.

Vienna wrinkled her brow. Was that an insult because I look like I need caffeine? To hell with him, she thought.

She didn't need to be insulted by some preppy guy. *Probably a snobby model,* she thought. *Or worse, maybe he's a movie star.* She wouldn't be surprised. A lot of movie stars lived in Palm Springs.

She tried to steal a sideways glance at him without him noticing. With her head turned to the side, as if she wanted to see out the window on the opposite side of the plane, she gazed at his strong cheekbones, straight nose, and perfectly proportioned features. She felt his good looks made him a bit more than intimidating.

Whatever, she thought. *I'm not here to impress anyone. At least it's a fairly short flight. I'll be out of here soon.*

She popped a handful of peanuts into her mouth and leaned over to grab her purse from beneath the seat in front of her. She dug out her iPod player, put her ear buds in and closed her eyes while listening to the latest music she'd recently downloaded from the Internet. Several songs later, she opened her eyes. The guy that had been sitting next to her was not in his seat, only his magazine. Not that she really cared where he was, but out of pure curiosity, she unlatched her seatbelt and stood up.

Stooped, so as not to bump her head on the overhead compartment, she glanced up and down the aisle. There was no sign of him. She surmised that he was probably in the bathroom. Why she was concerned, she wasn't quite sure.

Vienna grabbed the magazine that the man had been

reading and sat back down. She thumbed through the pages until she came to one that was dog-eared. She glanced at the items on the page, slippers, a watch, some kind of wallet, reading glasses and one of those hearing aid things that you plug into your ear to amplify sound while watching TV. The page opposite had the temperature-gauging mug and several other creative items.

Shrugging, Vienna placed the magazine back on the empty seat next to her. The last thing she needed was for that guy to return to his seat and see her looking at his magazine. She had her own copy in the back pocket of the seat in front of her. She wondered what kind of lame excuse she'd give him if he caught her. She'd probably just play dumb and pretend she didn't realize she already had a copy of that magazine and that she was curious to learn more about the temperature mug. Maybe her father would like one for his birthday. Or maybe she can give it to him as a peace offering when he sees his credit card bill.

Vienna turned in her seat and looked again for the guy that had been sitting next to her.

He wouldn't fall for her lame excuse as to why she was thumbing through his magazine. She figured he'd know the truth. He'd assume she was checking up on him. Then his already big head would swell even more thinking that she had a thing for him or something. He was the arrogant type, she could tell.

All she could think of now was how thankful she was that he hadn't caught her with his magazine. Or even worse, that he had caught her looking up and down the aisle of the plane for him. That would've been a little more than embarrassing.

Ugh, she scolded herself, *stop thinking about him. Just*

because he's handsome doesn't mean I need to go all gaga.

Leaning back her seat as far as it would recline, she turned her music back on, closed her eyes, and pretended she didn't care.

***

Vienna grabbed her duffle bag from the baggage claim and headed for the rent-a-car window. It was a good thing that she knew the Palm Springs area. Her father had a vacation home there. Being that it was a Thursday and also not a holiday weekend, she lucked out. She'd been able to purchase an inexpensive plane ticket, and reserve a small compact vehicle at the last second.

Sliding her credit card across the counter, she said a silent prayer that her father wouldn't notice her recent charges. She tried to keep them low to stay off what she called the Father radar. Her dad wasn't one to complain about how much she charged, but he would be a little concerned that she booked herself on a flight to Palm Springs in the middle of a college semester. However, it wasn't as if she couldn't do her homework or study from wherever she decided to go. As long as she could link up wirelessly, there wouldn't be any problems getting her homework done. Now days, there was no excuse for failing a class. She could even take her tests online.

The woman working the counter gave Vienna a form to fill out and asked her if she'd like to purchase insurance.

"That was a little too easy," Vienna breathed, as she stepped out the front doors of the airport a few minutes later. She waited outside until a man drove up with her rental, a cute little red convertible with tan interior.

Driving down Gene Autry to catch the 10 freeway, Vienna decided that she wasn't going to check into a hotel.

She'd head over to her father's vacation home instead. To smooth things over before he noticed her credit card charges, she'd give him a call and ask if it was okay if she stayed there for a while.

Vienna dialed her father and took in a couple of deep breaths as she listened to the phone ring through the portable Bluetooth she clipped to the visor.

"Damn," she muttered when she got his voicemail. In some ways, she was relieved because she could just leave a message and wouldn't have to listen to his lecture about being irresponsible. However, she didn't have a key or a way to let herself into his house.

"Hi Daddy," Vienna said, leaving a voicemail, her voice sweet and childlike. "I hope you don't mind, I've just been feeling a bit stressed out and needed to take a small break from school. No worries, I have my homework with me," she decided to throw in. "The reason why I'm calling is that I decided to take a short vacation in Palm Springs. Is it okay if I stay at your house? Thanks, Daddy. I love you."

Vienna took the freeway to the Monterey exit and drove until she got to the front gate of the country club where her dad's vacation home was located. It was one of several homes that her father had owned since she was a child. She, her brother, mother and father had spent many Christmas vacations in Palm Springs when she was little, well, up until her parent's divorce. Her parents had split up right before her thirteenth birthday. Talk about a wonderful welcome to teenage life.

Vienna rolled down her window, reached out and punched in the same code her dad used at all of the gated communities. When she punched in the pound key the gate slid open.

She followed the main street down to the very end and made a left turn then a right. The house looked exactly how she remembered it. The light beige stucco and reddish tile roof. The yard was a bit different though. Her dad must've had it re-landscaped since her last visit. After all, it had been a little while since her last visit. She, and her best friend, Kim, flew out once for spring break, and then later that same year, she, Kim, and her brother, Jared, flew out and met her dad during their winter break from school. Her dad came in from San Francisco where he resided most of the year, and she, Kim, and Jared flew in from Sacramento. Now her brother lives in Connecticut and attends Yale University. And she, well, she still lived in Sacramento, near her mother, and took classes at the state university and worked part time in an art studio teaching lessons to children. Her father wasn't entirely thrilled with her choices in life. Nevertheless, she couldn't help it, she was who she was. Not everyone was born to be someone brilliant and important.

Vienna sighed. She knew she wasn't even a talented artist. She was just an okay artist. Her father gave her the opportunity to attend a private art academy in San Francisco, but at the time, she turned it down. She told her father that she wasn't even sure if art was what she wanted to pursue. When in fact, at the time, the only thing she had cared to pursue was her boyfriend, Brandon, her first love. However, things didn't work out. And there was no way she would ever admit to her father that the only reason she had stayed in Sacramento and turned down the opportunity to go to a private art school was for a man. Therefore, she kept up the façade that she was

9

happy with her decisions and just kept plunging through life without any real direction. She just took life day by day and hoped that she was on the correct path.

Thinking of her failed relationship with Brandon made her stomach tie up in a knot. She never really did have good luck in that department. She even tried going out on blind dates with several different men, which her friends had set her up with, to try to ease her pain. None of those ended on a good note either.

Love bites, Vienna thought, while she pulled the red convertible into her father's driveway. She glanced at her cell phone. No missed calls. She wondered if she should try windows and doors to see if anything at her dad's house was unlocked. What if she accidentally set off the security alarm? Frowning, she was beginning to think that a hotel room would be the best choice for her.

For whatever reason, Vienna felt compelled to get out of her car and try the front door anyway. Walking up the cement path, Vienna stopped and stared at the colorful flowerbed with a look of puzzlement. There were garden gnomes of all shapes and sizes within the flowers.

Garden gnomes? she wondered. *Since when did dad buy garden gnomes?*

Vienna shook her head. She'd have to tease her father about whomever it was he hired to landscape. Obviously, he hadn't seen the place in a while. She couldn't imagine him being too happy about a bunch of gnomes taking residence in his petunias. Even the colorful array of flowers were a little over the top.

I mean, really, Vienna thought, garden gnomes in the desert? How silly was that?

She followed the cement path to the front porch and

up the three slab steps. On the corner of the porch was a white three-tier fountain with a chubby cupid at the top. Water streamed from the cupids bow and arrow. Next to the fountain was a white wrought-iron bench with a barrel of pink flowers next to it.

Her father used to have two black chairs and a small table with an ashtray on the front porch. It was his designated smoking area. Whenever they'd visit, her father would either sit on the front porch and smoke or sit next to the pool out back. She scanned the front porch for an ashtray. No ashtray.

Frowning, Vienna clutched the doorknob and stared down at a pink, heart-shaped welcome mat beneath her feet. Hearts, gnomes, and angel babies were not something she'd ever expect to see at her dad's house.

To her surprise, the door was unlocked.

Maybe my father is in town. Wouldn't that be ironic?

Stepping into the entrance hall she called out, "Dad? Dad?" Her voice echoed, bouncing off the high ceilings and paved cement floors. There was no answer. She walked over to the kitchen and set her black and silver purse on the grey speckled granite countertop. The stainless steel sink was full of dirty dishes.

"Dad?" she called out again. "It's me, Vienna!"

She heard thumps from upstairs, then light footsteps on the stairs. Vienna headed towards them.

"Hello? Dad?" she asked, peeking round the corner of the staircase.

"May I help you?" A woman wearing a skin tight T-shirt, hot pink stretch pants while carrying a tiny white dog in one arm was holding onto the railing, flouncing down the stairs.

11

Vienna was in shock. It took her a moment to find her voice. "I-uh-I'm looking for my dad."

"Your dad?" the woman asked. The dog squirmed and the woman cooed, "It's okay, Poopsie."

"This is my father's house," Vienna said.

The woman's eyes grew large. They glowed a brilliant turquoise blue against her dark tanned skin and bleach blonde hair. "Oh!" she said, "you're Paul's daughter. I almost forgot he had a daughter. How silly of me!"

Vienna smirked. *Paul's daughter? I'm probably the same age as you,* she thought.

Just then, Vienna's cell phone began to ring. She grabbed it from her purse on the counter. The caller ID said that it was her father.

"Hi Dad," she said, answering it. "Yes, I'm already here. No, actually, I'm at your house. Uh, huh. Yes, well, we already met. Uh, huh. Yes, Bunny seems very nice." Vienna shook her head and held the cell phone out to Bunny. "He wants to talk to you."

"Paul?" she said into the phone while setting Poopsie down on the floor. "No. No, she can stay with me. It's no problem. Of course, I'm sure."

Vienna put her hands out in front of her and began waving them in front of Bunny. She shook her head. There was no way she wanted to stay in her father's house with a blonde bimbo named Bunny.

Bunny batted her long thick lashes at Vienna. "Yes, I think it'll be good for us to bond."

Bond? Vienna wondered. *Why in the world would she want to do that?*

Vienna continued to try to get Bunny's attention. She snapped her fingers at her. When Bunny glanced at her again, Vienna mouthed the word *no* and shook her head.

"Of course, Paul. It'll be fun. We'll do girly things together. She could use a makeover. I know a wonderful beautician that can do wonders." She giggled. "All right, pumpkin-wumpkin, here let me give you back to her."

Vienna sighed and took the phone from Bunny. She threw Bunny a dirty look, which she either ignored or didn't seem to notice. Bunny batted her eyelashes, scooped up Poopsie from the floor, and held the little white fluff of fur close to her fake bosom.

"Pumpkin-wumpkin?" Vienna asked when she got on the phone. She couldn't imagine her mother ever calling him anything mushy like that.

Her dad chuckled, "Yes, it's a pet name she has for me."

"I see."

"You can stay in your usual room," he said. "Bunny's fine with that."

"No. No, Dad. Please, don't worry about it. I didn't realize you had company staying here. I'll go get a hotel room. It's no big deal. I should've made plans before coming out. It was silly of me to just show up."

"Bunny's not company," he said. "She's my girlfriend. She lives there."

"Oh. I see," Vienna said, walking away from Bunny who was now feeding Poopsie on the kitchen counter. "That explains the garden gnomes and the naked angel baby fountain on the front porch."

Her dad chuckled again, "Bunny loves those gnomes."

"Yeah, I can tell. Does Mom know about this?" Vienna whispered harshly while covering the phone with

13

her hand.

"Not yet. She'll be finding out soon enough," he said. "Bunny and I are getting married."

"What?" Vienna couldn't believe what she was hearing. Her mother and father had had an on again off again relationship since they divorced many moons ago. Even though they weren't together in a traditional sense, they sort of were a couple. They shared a strange love hate thing with each other. Vienna didn't want to be the one to break the news to her mother.

It's no wonder I can't find a decent relationship, she thought. *Look at my role models.*

"I want you to get to know Bunny," her father said. "This happens to be a perfect time for you to visit."

"Yeah, okay." Vienna was in shock, and not only because of the blonde bimbo named Bunny, but her father hadn't once mentioned school or berated her for not having had graduated yet, or for not having some kind of genius plan for her future.

"Good," he said after a moment of uncomfortable silence. "I'm glad that's settled."

"Sure."

"You two have a good time. Go shopping or do whatever it is you women do to bond. I want you to like your new stepmother."

Vienna began to choke. *Stepmother?* She cringed at the thought. *We could be sisters. Well, age wise, anyway.*

"Are you sick?"

Vienna coughed a bit more and then managed to croak, "Must be allergies."

"Ah, well, the desert in bloom. Happens every year, especially when there's a rainy winter."

14

"Uhmmm." Vienna cleared her throat.

"I might have some seasonal stuff in the cupboard."

"Okay, thanks."

"I'll be flying out next weekend. I'd like to be there this weekend, but I've got some work related things to take care of."

"Yeah, okay."

"Maybe you'll decide to stay a bit longer. Take a break from school. You deserve it."

"Yeah, maybe." Vienna wasn't sure how to reply to that. Who was this easy going man she was talking to and what had he done with her father?

"I need to get back to work now, okay, honey?"

"Yeah, okay."

"Love you."

"Yeah, love you, too." Vienna ended the call and scowled at her phone.

Chapter 2

After making herself comfortable in the room she'd always stayed in when visiting, she decided to take a shower while contemplating on what to do next.

The Village Fest Street Faire was laying heavily on her mind. Well, that and the fact that her dad was about to marry a woman who was actually named after a rodent. Okay, she knew that rabbits weren't really rodents. But, still, who in their right mind names their child Bunny? But then again, she was named after a hotel that her parents had stayed in on their honeymoon in Italy. And what made matters worse, she was also Italian. So who was she to talk?

Letting the warm water pour over her face she let it wash away the fears of her father making a terrible mistake. She tried to reason with herself that he was a grown man and he needed to make his own decisions. His love affairs were not her concern. She just needed to keep her mouth shut. Then her mind drifted to her mother. Oh, jeez, what would she tell her? She'd have to tell her something. If she didn't, her mother would want to know why she kept it from her when she found out about the marriage.

Don't think about it, she told herself. *Worry about it when the time comes. No sense in getting all worked up.*

She grabbed the shampoo bottle from the shelf in the corner of the shower and poured a decent sized amount into her hand. It was the awful 2 in 1 stuff. She forgot to pack her own. Massaging the shampoo into her scalp and working it into her locks, she hoped that she'd be able to get a brush through it later. Just then, the lights went out. The bathroom was black as pitch.

"What the heck?" Vienna muttered.

She began to rinse the shampoo from her hair while telling herself not to worry. She reasoned that the electricity would come on soon. And sure enough, the lights flickered on.

"See," she said out loud, "you almost panicked over nothing." But as soon as she said the words, the lights flickered and went off again. "You've got to be kidding me," she groaned, wishing the bathroom had a window to let in sunlight.

All of a sudden, an unfathomable fear welled up inside her chest. Despite the warm water running over her body, deep, cold chills swept through her, creating goose bumps on her arms and legs.

Over the drumming sound of the running water, she could hear squeaking in the darkness. It was a familiar sound, as if someone was running their fingertips against the mirror.

"Who's there?" she asked.

The squeaking stopped.

She listened. All she could hear was the falling of water splashing around her and nothing else.

The icy chill vanished.

"Hello? Someone in here?"

Still nothing.

Taking in a deep breath, she held it for a moment then slowly exhaled. Her breathing was loud in her ears. She stood still for a moment, but heard nothing out of the ordinary. The only sound was of the running water. She rationalized that she was spooking herself for no apparent reason. Kind of like she did when she was a child. She'd freak herself out over the dolls and stuffed animals in her room. From the shadows they created with the light of her nightlight, she'd swear she'd see them moving around her bedroom.

Overactive imagination, she reasoned. I have an overactive imagination. That's what my dad always said. Besides, who'd be in the bathroom with me? I would've noticed if the door opened and closed.

Grabbing the handle, Vienna turned the knob all the way to the left, switching off the shower. She waited for a moment and listened. Then, with another flicker, the lights turned back on.

Quickly, she stepped out onto the bathmat while drying her body off. When she finished, she leaned forward and wrapped her hair up in the towel by twisting it until it stayed in place. She realized she'd forgotten to turn the fan on and her skin was beginning to feel clammy and wet again. She could've sworn she'd switched it on before her shower.

Waving the steam away, she walked over to the light switch and turned on the fan. That's when she saw it. Her heart began to pound in her chest. Through the foggy, steamed up room, she could see the words HELP ME scribbled in the center of the mirror. Leaning closer to examine it, in her muddled, steamy reflection, a dark shadow came up behind her. Again, icy chills came out of nowhere and swept through her body, ripping through her stomach.

Vienna screamed.

Chapter 3

After feeling like an idiot, Vienna was now both dressed and quite embarrassed, sitting at the table in the eat-in kitchen. She stared out the bay window at the shimmering water of the swimming pool. Bunny brought her a can of diet soda and then sat down across from her. Poopsie was snuggled in her arms.

"I feel really stupid," Vienna said.

"Don't," Bunny said with the wave of a manicured hand. A flash of hot pink nails streaked through the air. "I would've freaked if the lights went out on me."

Vienna shook her head. "I don't get it. The electricity didn't go off down here?"

"Uh huh." Bunny shook her head. "I would've just died if the TV went off in the middle of my soaps. Do you watch Days?"

"Uh, no." Vienna steered the subject back on track. "Maybe there's something wrong with the wiring in the bathroom. I guess it could be rats or something. I heard squeaking. I know the desert has problems with them trying to escape the heat."

"It's not even that hot yet," Bunny explained.

"Yeah," Vienna agreed. "Guess not."

"We don't have rats," Bunny said to Poopsie. She held the little fluff-ball up so that their noses were touching. "So don't you worry, baby. Mommy would never let a rat in here. No, no, no."

"But that still doesn't explain the mirror," Vienna said, trying to sort out what had happened, ignoring Bunny and Poopsie.

Bunny shrugged, pulling Poopsie close to her chest. She scratched behind the little dog's ears. "Maybe it's been there for a long time. I'll have to make sure when the maid cleans she does the bathroom mirrors."

"Yeah, I guess so." Vienna frowned. "But why write that?"

"Could've been a joke," Bunny said. "Paul and I have had lots of company."

"Could be," Vienna said, and took a sip of soda. She didn't tell Bunny about the dark shadow that came up behind her in the bathroom. It had all happened so fast, she thought it was better to keep that to herself. She didn't want her dad's bimbo girlfriend to think she was a freak of nature. It was bad enough that Bunny thought her scream of terror was from being startled by the lights going out.

"You know, your brother came to visit," Bunny said. "I wouldn't be surprised if he wrote that just to tease whoever used the bathroom next."

That got Vienna's attention. "What? Jared came out to visit?"

"Oh, yes," Bunny said. "He's going to be Paul's best man at our wedding."

"Really," Vienna practically snorted. Jared hadn't

even bothered to tell her of their father's fiancé. Not that she and Jared were really close. However, she was still surprised that he hadn't at least warned her. It would've been nice to have known what was going on. But then again, he probably doesn't want to be the one to have to tell their mother about bimbo Bunny, either.

"So," Bunny said, setting Poopsie on the table in front of her. "How about we go have a girl's night out?"

"Oh," Vienna took a big gulp of soda, "Um, I don't know."

"Come on," she cooed. "It'll be fun. We can get all dressed up."

Vienna shrugged her shoulders. She sucked in air while trying to think of something nicer to say than no way in hell.

"I can fix your hair."

"Uh…" Vienna reached up and touched her still wet, unruly hair as she searched for an excuse then remembered her dream, the reason why she came to Palm Springs to begin with. "I plan on going to the Street Fair tonight," she blurted out.

"Oh! That'll be fun!" Bunny clapped her hands. "What a fantastic idea! We can go to the pub afterwards!"

"Uh…well…I…er…"

"You are old enough to drink, aren't you?"

"Um, yeah, but…"

"That settles it." She jumped up from the table and lifted little Poopsie into her arms. She said excitedly while leaving the room, "I'm going to go raid my closet. I'm sure I have something that'll fit you. I love girl's night out!"

Vienna tried to smile, but she knew she probably

looked more like she was constipated. "Goody, goody gumdrops," she muttered sarcastically. "Can't wait for all the fun to begin."

***

Tables, booths, and colorful umbrellas lined both sides of the main strip in Palm Springs. Every Thursday night, Palm Springs held what was called the Village Fest Street Faire. It was a tradition that had been going on for over sixteen years, rain or shine.

The main street, Palm Canyon Drive, in historic downtown Palm Springs was blocked off every Thursday evening from six to ten. Tourists from all over the country, better known as Snow Birds because they traditionally come to the desert to avoid cold winters, flocked to the popular tourist trap.

What Vienna liked most about the street fair was that all the items were handmade. Being an artist, she appreciated the hard work that went into the artisan's wares. From what she understood, each vendor had to go before a panel of judges prior to being accepted. Therefore, each booth contained unique items anywhere from pottery to soaps, candles to paintings, and original music sold by local musicians. And of course, there were also stands selling fruits and veggies, and other various food items for people with the munchies.

Vienna had fond memories of coming here as a child with her parents. The street fair had been a small event back then. Now, there were mobs of people, tons of booths, and many items for sale.

The overly excited Bunny dragged Vienna from booth to booth. So far, Bunny purchased two bracelets and some specialty soaps. Vienna couldn't help but

23

wonder whose money was being used to buy the items. Bunny's money or her father's? Not that it was any of her business.

"You should get something for yourself," Bunny said, looking at handmade leather purses. "These are adorable. Oh, look, its pink." She shifted Poopsie, who was in a turquoise blue dog carrier, to her other hand and lifted up a pink purse with black leather tassels to get a better look at it. "I could see you carrying this."

"You can?" Vienna scrunched up her nose. It wasn't her taste. Besides, even if it were, she wouldn't give Bunny the pleasure of knowing it.

"You'd look so cute with it!" she squealed.

Vienna shook her head. "I don't think so."

"Let me buy it for you," Bunny said.

"No, I really…"

"Please," she begged. "I really want to get you something. And it'll go good with jeans." Bunny ignored Vienna's protests and handed the purse to the vendor.

Vienna rolled her eyes and sighed. She didn't want Bunny buying her anything. The only reason she was out with Bunny to begin with was to humor her father.

Looking up and down the strip, Vienna was beginning to feel silly flying out to Palm Springs because of a stupid dream. Why she felt compelled to come here, she wasn't quite sure.

"Oh," Bunny said, clutching Vienna's arm. "You really need to hear this guy. He really is something. Your father loves him. I bought him one of his CDs."

She steered Vienna through the crowd of people until they reached a mob that formed around a musician dressed in a pirate costume, standing on a street corner at an intersection. The tunes of extraordinary new age music floated on the evening air from an electric cello he was playing. His audience stood very still, mesmerized by the enchanting show and mystical music.

A six foot something man dressed in drag, wearing a stunning yellow sequined gown with slits up the sides showing off his muscular thighs and a feathered headdress pushed in front of Vienna, momentarily distracting her. He was passing out flyers advertising some sort of impersonation show. "It's absolutely fabulous!" he crooned, handing a yellow flyer to Vienna. "Honey, you simply must see it. Our celebrity impersonators are the best in the desert."

"Thank you," Vienna said, glancing at the flyer, before folding it and slipping it into her purse.

He seems familiar, she thought, watching the elegantly dressed man glide through the crowd, flittering from person to person. She could've sworn she'd seen him somewhere before.

When she turned her attention back to the cello playing pirate who was finishing his song, she realized that she'd lost track of Bunny who was no longer at her side. Not that she really cared, but Bunny had insisted on driving tonight and Vienna was dependent on her for a ride home.

"Great," she muttered. "I lost the airhead."

Instead of staying put, she decided that the best thing to do would be to wander over to the nearest booth. If she continued to peruse the booths, she'd probably bump into Bunny. Worst case scenario, she'd go to that pub that Bunny had mentioned and see if she ended up there. And if not, well, she'd just have to call a cab and charge it to her father's card. If he asked, she'd just mention to him how his irresponsible girlfriend drove them to the street fair then lost her.

Vienna squeezed past a group of people purchasing the cello pirate's CD and walked up to a booth on the opposite side of the street. Unusual scents in gorgeous little bottles were on display. She sampled two or three different fragrances, dabbing them on her wrist, for lack of something better to do.

The last fragrance she tried was extremely sweet. It reminded her of cotton candy. A tag dangling from the red bottle said that if worn it would bring you love.

"That's the last thing I need," Vienna whispered. Out of the blue, she had the feeling she was being watched and glanced over her shoulder. No one seemed to be paying her any attention.

"I like that one," said a man's voice, startling her.

Vienna was astonished to see the good-looking man from the airplane, standing next to her, smiling. He nodded at the red bottle that she was still holding in her hand. "Smells nice."

Caught off guard, Vienna shrugged. "It's all right, I guess. Kind of sweet."

"Brings love," he said, picking up the little tag attached to the bottle, reading it.

"Yeah," she said, and then set the bottle back on the shelf. "Silly, huh?"

"Nothing silly about love," he said.

"Yeah, okay," she said sarcastically and laughed. "Didn't we meet on the plane?"

"We met long before that."

Vienna smirked. Was that a pick up line? How

cheesy was that? And was he actually using it on her? He was most definitely out of her league, so he probably didn't mean it in that way. Maybe she just reminded him of someone else and he truly believed that they'd met before.

"Well, okay…umm…" She glanced in the direction of the next booth.

"I'll come with you," he said, following her glance.

"Oh, uh…" Vienna wasn't used to a man being so forward. She was far from a beauty queen and wasn't quite sure how to react.

The man smiled. "If you don't mind, that is."

"Well, no." She shrugged. "I don't mind. I'm Vienna, by-the-way."

"I'm sorry. I should've introduced myself. Of course, you wouldn't remember me. I'm Jack." He held his hand out for her to take.

"Remember you?" Vienna asked. "I really don't think we've met before. I'm sure I'd remember you." She took his proffered hand and a bolt of electricity unlike anything she ever felt before shot through her arm and settled into a strange sort of tingle in her shoulder. Quickly she let go of his hand and stared at her palm. The shock wasn't painful or anything. In fact, it was quite the opposite. His electric touch left a feeling of warmth even though his skin was cold. It was a sensation that was hard to explain.

Jack was watching as Vienna examined her hand. When she noticed his blue eyes upon her, she crossed her arms over her chest, suddenly feeling a bit uncomfortable. "I-uh, I'm looking for my Dad's girlfriend. I kind of lost her."

"The blonde one," he said.

Vienna tilted her head. "Yeah," she said, a bit puzzled. "She's blonde."

"She's all right," he said. "She's picking up some strawberries from the Farmer's market."

"How'd you…?" Vienna's voice trailed off as they walked over to the next booth.

"I saw her with you," he said.

"Oh."

"She's the one with the dog," he said. "Stuffed in a blue bag."

"Yes," Vienna laughed. "That's her."

"He doesn't like it," Jack said.

"Doesn't like what?" Vienna stood in front of an oil painting of the desert in bloom. The flowers were so rich and colorful. Even on her best days, her paintings were never as detailed.

"The dog," Jack said. "He doesn't like the bag."

"I'm sure he doesn't," Vienna said and shook her head. What a strange thing to say, she thought. He sounds so serious about it. She turned her attention back to the artwork on display.

"So what do you think of this one?" she asked, pointing to a painting of a basket of fruit. She liked the simplicity of the painting. Yet at the same time, the detail in each piece of fruit was so in depth that it looked like a photograph.

When Jack didn't answer, she turned around. He was gone. Puzzled, she looked all around her. He wasn't anywhere to be seen. An older couple came up behind her to admire the painting.

"Excuse me," Vienna said softly, ducking out of their way.

"No problem, dear," the white haired woman said, then stated to her husband while clutching his arm, "Arnold, this is a lovely painting. I think it would look nice in our dining room."

"Wouldn't you rather have something more like that?" He nodded to the painting next to it. "A desert picture would be more appropriate."

"Just because our house is in the desert doesn't mean that all the paintings have to be of the desert," she scowled. "You have no sense of style."

"Sense of style?" he huffed. "I have plenty of…"

"Um, excuse me," Vienna butted in. "Sorry to interrupt. But you didn't by any chance see where the man that was standing next to me went?"

The old couple looked at each other. "I didn't see anyone. Did you, Arnold?"

"No, Harriett. I didn't notice anyone."

"Oh, okay," Vienna said. "Thanks."

She looked around again but didn't see Jack or Bunny. She left the display of oil paintings, joined the throngs of people in the street, and walked along the booths, but she wasn't paying attention to their wares. Instead, her mind was on other things, like Jack.

What an odd encounter that was, she thought. He seemed to be into her. Or at least she thought he was, with the way he was flirting and all, and then the first chance he got, he bolted.

Vienna continued to walk until she reached the end of the street fair. White wooden blockades with orange reflecting stripes marked the end, blocking the street from cars. She wandered past the barricade, passing a couple of restaurants on her left with outdoor seating and live music, one being the Village Pub that Bunny had mentioned, and walked until she reached a block where the music suddenly faded into the distance, the chatter of people disappeared, and silence enveloped her.

She continued to walk alone down the dark, quiet street. She wasn't sure where she was going. All she knew was that it felt right. As if something was leading her, telling her this was where she was supposed to go.

Passing the dark shops, all of them closed for the night, she wandered until she reached an intersection. She stopped at a crosswalk, and then decided to hang a left. No one was around. Not even a vehicle was in sight. She then stopped in front of a dark alley and stood there. Squinting, she could just make out the outline of a dumpster between the buildings. There were no street lamps, no security lights, just a trickle of moonlight streaming in between the rooftops into the alleyway.

Breaking the silence, glass hit the ground and shattered by the dumpster. Vienna jumped, her heart raced with fear, but she continued to stand there, staring into the alley. Something was beckoning to her to enter the darkness.

Something moved. She saw it from the corner of her eye. A dark figure slipped into the slit of moonlight and then quickly out of it. Vienna entered the alley. She took careful, silent steps, following the sliver of light over to the dumpster where she saw the odd shadow appear then disappear. The gut wrenching feeling that was calling her, leading her to this place became stronger, deeper, harder to resist. It was as if she were in a trance and not in control of her actions. She had to follow it. She took a couple more steps forward.

Something crunched beneath her shoes. Vienna rested her hand on the dumpster to balance as she lifted her foot. Glass stuck within the grooves of her tennis shoe and glittered in the silver moonlight.

A whoosh of icy air came out of nowhere and blasted Vienna, blowing her hair away from her face. Gripping the side of the dumpster, feeling the metal hard against her palms, Vienna resisted the urge to run. Blackness took over and within her head, she could see the face of a dark haired girl. A sudden flash of red. A wave of dizziness. The nightmare.

A scream rang in her ears, and terror gripped her from within.

Chapter 4

"Are you all right?"

Her head pounded as if she'd been pummeled by a jackhammer.

"Vienna, can you hear me? Vienna?"

"Hmmm." Vienna's lips wouldn't move. She couldn't seem to form words.

"Vienna?"

With all her strength, Vienna lifted her eyelids. A dark blurry form leaned over her. She squeezed her eyes closed against the raging headache.

"Are you all right?"

"Yeah, yeah," she mumbled, using her elbows to help prop herself up. She was in the alley, lying on the cold ground. It was still dark out. "Jack?" she asked, making out his silhouette in the moonlight.

"What happened?" he asked.

"I-uh-I don't know," Vienna said, sitting up. She pushed her fingertips to her temples. "I've got a really bad headache. I think I might have hit my head."

"Do you need to go to a hospital?"

"No," she said, shaking her head. "But something

weird happened. I saw this girl."

"A girl?"

"This may sound strange, but..." her voice trailed off.

"But what?"

"You'll think I'm crazy. Never mind," she said, shaking her head, again. "It's nothing."

"Try me," Jack said, crouched down next to her. He grasped her hand.

Vienna felt a strange pulsing sensation within his palm, but this time she didn't pull away. She let the warm tingling sensation pulse up her arm. Her headache began to subside.

"The girl," she said. "I think she was murdered."

"Murdered?" he asked.

"Yes, right here." She frowned trying to make sense of the ridiculous words coming from her own mouth. "She died right here. Bled to death. I can feel her."

Jack was quiet for a moment. He stayed crouched by Vienna's side, holding her hand. Finally he spoke, "Here, let me help you up." He stood, now holding both her hands; he pulled her to her feet.

Feeling a rush of dizziness, Vienna leaned against him for support. She hoped she wouldn't throw up. Jack gently touched Vienna's forehead. His fingers were cold and icy, but regardless, his touch filled her with warmth. Her dizziness subsided.

"Do you know the girl's name?" he asked.

"No," she said, her voice barely a whisper. "You believe me?"

"Of course, I do." He steered her out of the alley and back onto Palm Canyon drive. They walked together in silence. The street fair had been packed up some time ago. The streets were quiet except for live music coming from a few late night bars along the strip.

Jack led Vienna to the pub and stopped at the black iron fence surrounding an outdoor bar. A worried looking Bunny sat at a table alone. Her forehead was creased with worry lines. She stared out at the street. She took a sip from a glass of ice water then looked up. Her eyes focused on Vienna's and lit up. She hopped up from the small table and ran to the entrance where Vienna stood. To get out the door, she pushed past several young men who were ogling at her.

"Where have you been?" she asked, hugging Vienna. "I've looked everywhere for you. I even called your father to see if he heard from you."

"Oh, no. You didn't," Vienna sighed, her shoulders slumped. "Why'd you call him?"

Bunny undid the death grip on Vienna and looked at her closely. "Oh my God, what happened to you? I didn't notice it at first, but you're a mess! Were you mugged? No one did anything to you, did they? Look at your hair. And your glasses, they're bent out of shape."

"I just kind of tripped and fell and hit my head," Vienna said. "I've always been a bit of a klutz." She wrinkled her nose, realizing for the first time that her glasses were on crooked. "My friend Jack found me."

"Jack?" Bunny asked, still looking Vienna up and down with a look of concern.

"Yeah," Vienna said, then realizing that Jack had disappeared again. "He was here just a second ago." She looked around. "You didn't see him?"

Bunny shook her head. "At least you're all right. That's all that matters. I'll call your father and let him know." She opened her purse and pulled out her pink rhinestone covered cell phone.

After Vienna talked to her father, explaining to him repeatedly that she was fine and didn't need to go to the hospital, he finally gave in and told her if she wasn't feeling well in the morning that Bunny had strict instructions to take her to the emergency room. Vienna agreed to go if she didn't feel well in the morning. Once the painful conversation was over, she, Bunny, and Poopsie who was sleeping in his turquoise bag, piled into the car and headed home.

The drive back to the house was quiet and uneventful which Vienna was thankful for. Her mind kept going over what had happened to her by that dumpster. She wasn't quite sure what did happen.

Was she delusional? Did she really trip and hit her head? She was beginning to wonder. But deep down inside she knew the truth. She hadn't been imagining things. She really did feel a presence of a girl. In fact, she could still feel the terror that the girl had felt. She was positive that a girl had been murdered there. But why would she know that and how? Why is it she could see the girl's frightened face and feel her panic?

Vienna's thoughts drifted to Jack. Now that was another question all together. This handsome, gorgeous guy from the airplane with the most beautiful deep blue eyes she'd ever seen flirts with her at the street fair and goes as far as walking around with her, then moments later, disappears.

What's up with that? And was it just pure luck that he happened to find her in that deserted dark alley? Had he been looking for her when she lost him at the booth with the oil paintings? Or maybe he followed her there. What kind of game was he playing? He disappeared on her again when they reached the pub. What's up with that?

Vienna continued to wonder about Jack until she found herself in her bed, her eyes heavy with exhaustion. The last thought that passed through her mind was an irrational one.

A thought that she'd never admit to having, not even to herself. She wondered what Jack's lips would feel like pressed against hers.

Friday, May 13
Chapter 5

Jack appeared in front of a coffee shop that was located in an outdoor shopping mall called The River, located in Rancho Mirage. He stared through a glass door and spied Vienna at the counter, ordering.

Glancing at a clock on the wall near the counter, he double-checked the time. It was ten in the morning. Therefore, it was still time for breakfast. Going from an existence where time doesn't exist to a world where time means everything was extremely stressful on him. Everything on the earth plane was monitored by time and adapting to time constraints wasn't always easy.

He toyed with the idea of coming back later. Coming on too strong would only cause Vienna to shut him out. Then again, right now, she needed him, even though she didn't know it. And it was his job to help keep her on track.

Jack concentrated on his available energy, conjuring it into his hand and fingers making them corporeal. He pulled open the glass door, a string of bells tied to the handle, jingled as he entered the shop. He walked up to the counter and checked out the menu scribbled on a whiteboard behind it. He watched as Vienna paid for her coffee and muffin and moved over to the part of the counter designated for picking up the order when it was ready.

Vienna leaned on the countertop watching the redheaded girl with her hair pulled up into curly pigtails; pour coffee into a Styrofoam cup. The girl snapped on a plastic lid and slid it across the counter to Vienna.

"I also ordered a muffin," Vienna told the girl.

"What kind?" she asked, wrinkling her tiny freckled nose.

"Banana nut," Vienna answered, curtly.

"Oh," the girl said looking perplexed. She leaned over and whispered to the black-haired girl who was working the cash register. They exchanged words then the girl returned to Vienna. "Sorry. We're out. Would you like something else?"

Tucking a loose strand of dark wavy hair behind her ear, Vienna glanced at the menu scribbled on the whiteboard while gnawing on her bottom lip. "Oh, I don't know. I guess blueberry will be fine."

"Okay," the girl said. She retrieved one from beneath the counter and placed it in a paper bag. "Sorry about the mix up."

"Do you have any cream and sugar?" Vienna asked while checking her bag to make sure she had a blueberry muffin in there and not bran or something else entirely.

"Over there," the girl said, nodding in the direction of a counter against the wall lined with containers of condiments, two napkins holders, and bins of plastic utensils.

"Thanks," Vienna muttered. She turned around, glanced over the rims of her glasses, and made eye contact with Jack. Instead of acknowledging him, she turned on the heel of her black shoes, and headed for the condiment counter.

Jack was a bit confused by Vienna's reaction. Or lack of reaction. He wondered if she hadn't seen him. He followed her over to the counter and waited for her to turn around again. When she did, she walked right past him and out the door.

Puzzled, Jack stared at her back as she walked away from the coffee shop. He closed his eyes, mustered up his energy and concentrated. Within a blink of an eye, he rematerialized on the sidewalk in front of a roaring fountain. The moisture in the air from the manmade river that ran through the shopping center, the fountains, and the misters that lined the buildings to make the desert more comfortable for the outdoor shoppers, made his transition from his dimension to this one, a bit easier. The coffee shop Vienna had been in only moments ago was around the corner from where he was now standing. He shielded his eyes from the brilliant desert sun that was hot even in the spring and could see Vienna headed in his direction.

Jack stood in Vienna's direct line of sight and raised his hand in a wave to get her attention. There was no possible way that she could miss him. He knew she could see him. She was naturally tuned to his energy waves whether she wanted to be or not. Instead of stopping, Vienna walked past him. Again, she gave no sign that she'd even seen him.

"Vienna," he called, trying to catch up with her. "Vienna, it's me Jack." His energy was feeling low. The air of the desert was so dry it was zapping his strength. He'd need to wait until nightfall when the air, even in the desert, moistened at least a little. He couldn't help but wonder if she'd built up a wall, a barrier between her dimension and his so that she couldn't see him.

***

What is up with that guy? Vienna thought, angrily. Can't he take a hint? I'm not interested. He needs to just go away. Men like him think they can just smile and turn on the charm and get their way with any woman. Well, I'm not that easy. He can't just flash me his pearly whites and expect me to swoon over him.

Vienna was still upset with Jack's little disappearing act last night. Even though she knew she should be grateful that he found her in that alley, she was angry with him instead. She knew her feelings were irrational, but she couldn't help it. She blamed him for what had happened to her. If he hadn't disappeared, then she wouldn't have felt compelled to go for a walk. And she wouldn't have seen that girl by the dumpster.

Or tripped, hit her head, and then imagined she'd seen that girl, she told herself.

"Who the heck does he think he is?" Vienna fumed, stomping back to her car in the parking lot. "Some nerve trying to talk to me. What a jerk!"

She couldn't stand self-assured men that believed they were some kind of Don Juan who could dazzle a girl with good looks and charisma. As far as she was concerned, he was one of those guys.

Turning the key in the ignition of her rental car,

Vienna suddenly wondered how Jack knew to look for her at The River. The desert was small, but not that small. Him being at the same coffee shop this morning had to be an odd coincidence. Either that or he was following her.

Unless, of course, Bunny told him where to look for her. As she dashed out of the house this morning, she shouted to Bunny from downstairs that she was going out for coffee. Not that Jack would even know where and how to reach Bunny to find out.

Or did he? Maybe he and Bunny knew each other.

She thought that would really be something to find out that Jack and Bunny was once an item. That would make perfect sense as to why he had disappeared last night when he walked her back to the pub. If he and Bunny used to date, and it had ended badly, he wouldn't want to talk to her.

Backing out of the parking space, Vienna glanced in her rearview mirror to make sure Jack wasn't following her. She had the strange feeling that she was being watched. Chills came out of nowhere and swirled between her shoulder blades. The little hairs on the back of her neck stood on end.

In the reflection of her rearview mirror, the dark despondent eyes of a girl were staring at her. Startled, she gasped and slammed her foot down hard on the brakes causing the car to jerk. Turning in the driver's seat, Vienna checked the backseat.

No one was there.

She looked again in her rearview mirror. Only her own eyes, shielded behind prescription sunglasses, were staring back at her.

HONK! An impatient woman behind the wheel of a

Silver Mercedes was honking at her to get out of the way.

"Sorry," Vienna muttered sheepishly and pulled back into her parking space to let the Mercedes pass. Her heart was pounding hard in her chest and strumming in her ears.

Those eyes, she thought, those deep brown eyes.

She knew she'd never forget them. Those eyes belonged to the girl she saw last night. The girl she thought she saw in the alley. She was sure of it.

***

Vienna spent the afternoon at the Westfield Mall in Palm Desert for lack of anything better to do. She wasn't quite sure what was happening to her or how to handle it. She thought that maybe shopping would give her time to think while being amongst normal, everyday people.

It was now late in the afternoon and she'd had a phone call from her father who berated her for not checking in with Bunny. Supposedly, Bunny was racked with worry.

Vienna protested that she was an adult and no longer a child needing to explain her whereabouts. Quickly her father backed off since he wanted her to like his soon-to-be-wife. He immediately dropped the lecture and told her to enjoy her day out shopping and to use his credit card to buy herself an outfit or two.

As much as Vienna disliked Bunny, she had to admit, her father having a fiancé wasn't all that bad. He seemed much more laid back. Not the uptight dad she was used to having.

Then, not even a half hour after her conversation with her father, she received a second phone call while she was trying on shoes. This one was from her mother. She tried to keep her father's blonde bimbo girlfriend out of

42

the conversation, but unfortunately, word had already gotten around to her mom through the social grapevine.

"I know," Vienna said, holding her cell phone to her ear while trying on a pair of black strappy sandals. "It came as a shock to me, too."

"Why didn't you call me?" Vienna's mother, Charlotte, asked.

"Mom," Vienna groaned, putting the sandals back in the shoebox. She leaned back in the red puffy chair. "I just found out yesterday when I got here. I hadn't a clue."

Charlotte sighed. "What's she like? I heard she's half his age."

"I don't know how old she is," Vienna said, trying to stay neutral. She didn't want to be in the middle of her parents' affairs.

"What does she look like?"

"Mom," Vienna groaned again, while putting her own shoes back on.

"What?" Charlotte snapped. "It's a perfectly reasonable question. I mean…"

"She's okay," Vienna said. "Blonde, kind of tall…"

"Is she thinner than I am?" Charlotte asked. "She probably is. Your father likes them thin. How big are her thighs? I bet she's never had children. Do you know how much weight I put on after having both you and your brother? Even liposuction couldn't keep the fat away. Just keeps coming back. And don't even get me started on the loose skin and stretch marks. So, does she have kids?"

"No, I don't think so."

"Well, in that case she's probably as skinny as a rail. I figured as much. Just like your father to find a skinny woman."

"She's got some weight on her," Vienna said, thinking of Bunny's enormous fake bosom. She just left out where her weight was distributed. "Oh, and she has a dog," she added, knowing her mother's love for animals.

"Oh," she said, glumly. "Well, I guess she can't be all that bad if she's got a dog. Figures."

"She seems okay," Vienna said again, trying to stay neutral. Bunny wasn't her favorite person, but at the same time, she didn't want to betray her father. And she most definitely didn't want to hurt her mother by admitting that Bunny was gorgeous.

"Well, tell your father I'm happy for him. I truly am."

"Okay, Mom. I'll tell him when I talk to him again. I love you."

"I love you, too, honey. I'd better get back to work. I have a house to show and I can see my clients coming up the walk way."

Vienna took in a deep breath then exhaled. That went a lot better than she had expected. Her mother was a Real Estate Agent and she loved her job. That was the only thing that kept her focused.

After all these years, Vienna knew her mother was still in love with her father. They just couldn't live with each other. They were both too independent and head strong which caused them to constantly argue whenever they were together. They never could agree on anything in life except for the fact that they couldn't be together.

Vienna was thankful that her mother loved her career and was keeping busy with work. She hoped that her work would help with the sting of finding out about Bunny. She knew her mother was hurting inside and wished she could help her find Mr. Right.

Vienna slipped her cell phone into her purse when it rang again. She stared at the screen and flinched. It was the art studio where she taught painting lessons. She'd forgotten all about calling in sick.

"Hello," Vienna said, weakly into the phone. She hoped the blaring music and noisy chattering of shoppers didn't carry through on the cell phone.

"Vienna, it's me."

Vienna relaxed. It was her best friend. "Oh, hi, Kim."

"Are you at a mall?" Kim asked.

"How can you tell?"

"Pleeease, do you really need to ask?" Kim loved to shop. She was always brandishing a new outfit.

Vienna laughed. "I'm sorry I forgot to call," she said, feeling awful about not having confided in her friend about her last minute plans. She just felt embarrassed about why she was in Palm Springs and didn't know how to explain it to anyone. Nothing made sense.

"No prob," Kim said. "I understand. So, what's the sale? It must be worth it. Whatever it is, you need to buy me one. No, wait. Make it two."

"Actually I'm at the mall in Palm Desert."

Kim had been there a couple of times before with Vienna.

"Palm Desert?" Kim asked. "That's a long way to go for a sale, even for a professional shopper like me. Why are you there? What's wrong?"

"Nothing's wrong. I just needed to get away."

"Vienna," Kim said. "I'm your closet and dearest friend. I'm hurt that you're not confiding in me. What's wrong? I know something's wrong. I can hear it in your voice."

"It's nothing…"

Kim continued, "I'm such a good friend that I am taking over the class today all by myself."

"I know. And I appreciate it. I really do."

"Well," Kim sighed, "just remember I'm here for you if you need to talk. Okay?"

"I know," Vienna said. "Thank you."

"Are you there because of a guy?"

"What?" The question threw Vienna for a loop. She hadn't expected it. She should've though. Kim loved men almost as much as she loved shopping and art.

"Never mind," Kim said. "I was hoping that since you were being so secretive you'd at least have a good reason. If it's not shopping or a guy, I mean, what else is there?"

"There was a really good looking guy on the plane," Vienna offered, hoping to feed her friend something juicy.

"Oh, really," Kim said, her voice perking up with interest. "Did you talk to him? What did he look like?"

"I talked to him," Vienna said. "His name is Jack. I ran into him again last night at the street fair. We walked around a bit."

"Ooooh, tell me more."

"There's not much more to say. He seemed nice enough at first, and then he just kind of ditched me. Didn't even say goodbye."

"Did he ditch you for his friends or for another girl?"

"I don't know. He just kinda disappeared. It was really weird."

"What a jerk!" Kim seethed. "The good looking ones usually are."

"Yeah, I guess so." Vienna decided to leave out the alley incident. Goose bumps emerged on her arms as she thought about it. "And actually I'm here spending some time getting to know my dad's fiancé, if you must know."

"Your dad's getting married?"

"Yup."

"Since when?"

"I just found out."

"That's crazy! So what's the stepmother like?"

Vienna cringed. The thought of Bunny being her stepmother made her stomach turn. "Bunny's okay."

"Bunny?" Kim asked. "You've got to be kidding. Her name is Bunny?"

"Yup."

"Wow." Vienna could hear Kim turn her attention to someone else. "Oh, hi, Tim, go get some paints and start setting up."

"I'll let you go," Vienna offered.

"Yeah, the class is coming in," Kim said. "Remember, you owe me big time. Are you gonna be out all week?"

"Yeah, looks that way. But I'll let you know. I might come back sooner."

"Okay. Buy me something nice. I'll call you later."

Vienna shook her head and touched the red telephone symbol on the touch screen ending the call. Just then, the phone vibrated. She was receiving a new text message.

"Now what," she mumbled, touching the message icon, opening it. A yellow bubble shape with a message popped up on the screen.

"Vienna, Please don't shut me out. I need to talk to

you. There are things you need to know. Jack"

"What the…?" Vienna looked all around her. She
had the dreaded feeling she was being followed. She
wondered how Jack got her phone number. She didn't
recall giving it to him last night. Or did she? Who knows?
Maybe she did. Nothing was making any sense.

She touched the information section of the text to see
what phone number it came from. No phone number was
attached. Very odd. Maybe the number was blocked. But
shouldn't it say it was from a blocked number? Instead,
there was no information at all. Only the name, Jack, was
on the phone number line and the date at the top of the
screen, reminding her that it was Friday the 13th. How
appropriate, she thought. Her life was getting weirder and
weirder.

Vienna looked up from her phone and noticed the
woman working in the shoe department staring at her. She
was probably waiting for her to steal something. Vienna
slid her phone back into her purse and got up to leave.
Fleeing the department store, and reentering the mall, she
turned and looked over her shoulder every few minutes to
make sure she wasn't being followed by Jack.

***

She thinks I'm good looking, Jack thought smugly to
himself, after eavesdropping on Vienna's phone
conversation with Kim. Feeling a bit arrogant, he smiled
while he continued to follow Vienna throughout the mall.

After a while, Jack's smugness was dwindling. In fact,
he was beginning to feel aggravated because at the
moment, he couldn't materialize. It zapped too much
energy from him to materialize fully so that the average
person on the earth plane could hear and see him. And

48

for the time being, he was too weak to reappear in physical form even for a little bit. Therefore, he was waiting for Vienna to take notice of him. He was reserving his energy, and only using it sparingly here and there. He wished that Vienna would stop being so stubborn and tune into his existence. He knew that if she wanted to, she could see him in his in-between state because of her heightened sense of awareness.

Jack watched Vienna glance worriedly over her shoulder. He knew she was confused about the changes occurring in her life. If she'd only give him the time of day, he'd be able to explain. Or at least try to explain. He knew that in a human body, only a small portion of the brain was used. What he had to tell her might be more than she could understand at first.

Vienna fled the mall to the parking garage in search of her rental car. Jack knew she could sense his presence because she was still nervously looking around.

Vienna scuttled through the lot, down a row of cars until she reached the convertible. Since she had the top up, she unlocked the doors with the button on the alarm. She really wanted to take the top down for the ride back to her father's house because the weather was so nice, but thought that would probably be a bad idea if she were being followed. She wanted to be as inconspicuous as possible. Not that a screaming red convertible helped her situation any.

Vienna looked intently in the direction of the mall, one more time. No one seemed to be paying her any attention. She hopped into the car, strapped herself in and switched on the ignition. She put the vehicle in reverse, and her eyes glanced to the rearview mirror. Stopping herself, she flicked the mirror away from her.

"Oh, no you don't," she said, remembering those dark soulful eyes that had stared at her earlier today. In her mind, she felt she was being silly, but refused to look in any of the mirrors anyhow. She used the controls on her armrest to adjust the side view mirrors to face away from her. She'd avoid all the mirrors while driving. The last thing she wanted was to have a car accident because she was imagining things.

"I'll just have to do this the old fashioned way," Vienna said, gripping her steering wheel, turning in her seat and staring out the back windshield while inching backwards from her spot.

Jack sat in the passenger seat watching Vienna. She was becoming both paranoid and close-minded. He had been afraid that this would happen. Her reaction to the changes in her life was far worse than he had imagined. He waved his hands in front of her face as she was backing up. She didn't even flinch.

When Vienna had seen Jack on the airplane, he was in an in-between state and was visible to her. She had had no problem seeing him. Therefore, he knew if she wanted to, she'd be able to see him right now. However, unconsciously, she'd built a thick wall of protection around herself, blocking him out. How would he ever get through to her with the importance of her mission?

"Vienna, let me in," he said. "It's me, Jack."

Vienna turned on the radio and began channel surfing in search of a decent radio station.

Jack touched the stereo and sent a small zap through the speakers making a crackling noise. Vienna pouted and tried another station.

Jack touched the stereo again, making the music crackle with static.

"Stupid car," Vienna hissed. "Can't get a decent signal." She turned the knob again and stopped on a country station. "I should've hooked up my iPod player." She pictured the iPod player in her room on the bed next to her laptop.

"Oh, come on!" Jack fussed. "You are being so pig headed! Has anyone ever told you that?"

"Once or twice," Vienna answered, and then turned up the volume on the radio.

Jack was stunned. He didn't expect her to answer him. "Did you just answer me?"

Vienna began to sing, Honky Tonk Badonkadonk.

"Vienna," he said. "Vienna! Can you hear me? Hello?"

Vienna groaned and lowered the volume on the stereo. "Great," she moaned. "Now I'm hearing voices. What the heck is wrong with me?" She stuck a finger in her ear right ear and vigorously wiggled it.

"Nothing's wrong with you," Jack answered, pleased to be finally getting through to her. "Just listen to me. Please."

Vienna glanced at the passenger seat, and then looked over her shoulder. "I swear I'm losing my mind," she mumbled and turned up the volume on the stereo. She sang at the top of her lungs to drown out any unwanted voices.

Chapter 6

The rest of the day was a bit uneventful. Vienna plugged in her laptop and took her art history course, her algebra two class, and then listened to her biology lecture online. She spent several hours taking notes on her classes. When she'd finally finished, it was growing dark outside and she was starving. She skipped down the stairs and headed for the kitchen. To her dismay, the fridge was stocked full of veggies, low fat yogurt, and tofu. No sodas and no junk food insight. She must've drunk the only diet soda in the house, yesterday. She snatched a bottle of spring water and opted for a carrot stick to calm her growling stomach until she could think of something better to eat.

"Wanna go out?" Bunny asked, from the couch. Vienna hadn't even noticed her in the living room. Bunny was sprawled out on the sofa, reading a book.

"No," Vienna lied. She wanted to go out, but not with Bunny. "I have a lot of homework."

"What are you taking?" Bunny asked, petting Poopsie who was curled up on her lap.

"I'm an art major," Vienna said.

"Art," Bunny said. "How interesting! I can't even draw stick figures." She giggled. "I was a boring Economics major."

Vienna's eyes popped open with surprise. That was the last thing she expected to hear out of Bunny's mouth. "Really? Economics?"

Bunny giggled again. "Don't look so surprised!" She waved her hand. "Everyone always looks surprised."

"Did you get your degree?" After the words flew out of Vienna's mouth, she felt embarrassed. She shouldn't have asked it that way.

"Actually," Bunny said. "I couldn't make up my mind, so I had a double major. I wanted to be an interior designer and my parents wanted me to be more studious. So I majored in Economics and in Interior Design. And guess what?"

"What?"

"I never used either," she laughed. "I was top of my graduating class and where did that get me? A job as a waitress."

"I see," Vienna said, not knowing how to react. "I'm sorry."

"Don't be sorry," she said. "If I weren't waitressing, then I wouldn't have met your father."

"Oh," Vienna said. "I didn't know."

Bunny smiled. "He's the best thing that has ever happened to me."

Vienna forced a smile. She probably looked a bit like the Cheshire cat right about now, all gums and teeth. "Do you still work as a waitress?" Vienna asked, twisting the cap off the bottle of water.

"No," Bunny said. "Paul doesn't like me waitressing."

"Oh," Vienna said, coughing. "Why?"

"He's a bit on the jealous side," Bunny said. "But that's okay. I'm using my free time to freshen up my interior design skills."

Hearing about her father in the sense of a jealous boyfriend, made Vienna feel uncomfortable. She'd never thought of him in that type of capacity. It was just too weird to think about. This was not the kind of conversation she wished to be having.

"Oh, okay," Vienna said. She turned to escape the room, but Bunny was too quick for her.

"How about pizza?"

Vienna stopped in her tracks. She had one foot on the bottom stair and her stomach lurched at the thought of pizza. "Sure," she said, appeasing her stomach. "Pizza sounds good."

"Oh, yea!" Bunny clapped her hands. "We can watch chick flicks and eat pizza! This will be so much fun! Do you like pepperoni?"

Vienna cringed. Chick flicks with Bunny sounded like total and utter torture. "Sure." Somehow, she managed to make her voice sound light and upbeat. Maybe she'd fly home tomorrow. She wasn't sure how much more of this she could take. The whole reason she flew out here anyway was because of a stupid dream. She wasn't here to appease her father by spending time with his fiancé that she didn't even know he'd had to begin with.

In fact, she was a little worried that she wouldn't be able to hold her tongue for much longer and she might accidentally say something rude and unforgiveable to Bunny.

"Okay, well, I don't like pepperoni or meat, so I'll order a vegetarian pizza for me and a pepperoni for you."

Vienna shrugged. "It really doesn't matter. I can eat vegetarian."

"Oh, goodie," Bunny said, batting her lashes. "You really shouldn't eat meat if you can help it. And if you're going to it should be free range. Right, Poopsie Woopsie?" She held Poopsie up so that they were touching noses. Poopsie licked his lips.

"Is he vegetarian, too?" Vienna asked.

"What? Who? Poopsie?" Bunny laughed. "Oh, no. Of course not. Don't be silly. He's a dog."

"Yeah, okay." Vienna made a face, but Bunny didn't seem to notice.

"You go finish up your school work and I'll order dinner."

"Great," Vienna mumbled and shot up the stairs.

***

After dinner and a two-hour sappy movie, Vienna made desperate excuses and headed upstairs to her room. She left a sobbing Bunny on the couch with half a box of tissue. Bunny had cried and awed over every touching line in the movie making it extremely difficult to concentrate. She kept weeping and saying repeatedly, "How sweet! That is so sweet!"

When the movie finally ended, Bunny slipped the next movie from her stack of DVDs into the player. That's when Vienna stretched, yawned, and excused herself from the room. She could only imagine how much tissue Bunny would go through while watching Titanic.

Lying across the bed, Vienna turned on her laptop and waited for it to boot up. The flashing of headlights streamed into the bedroom from outside, lighting up the semi-dark room. The blinds were still open and all of the sudden, Vienna had the eerie feeling that someone was standing outside in the dark, watching her. She got up, walked over to the window, and peered out at the street in front of the house. It was vacant. The neighborhood was quiet. No one was about. She twisted the wand, closing the blinds, and returned to her computer. The strange feeling had to be her imagination again. That's what she told herself and shoved the thought to the back of her mind.

Vienna sat back down on the bed, and with a flick of her mouse, clicked on the email icon. Nothing new was in her inbox. She then checked her spam. She scrolled down the list, deleted several emails from stores announcing their last minute sales, and stopped when she came to an unmarked message. She wondered if she should open it. Sometimes legit mail accidentally got filtered into her spam folder.

She wondered if the email was important. She didn't want to delete it without at least opening it. But then again, what if it really was spam and it had some horrible computer virus attached to it? Her last computer had gotten a Trojan and she eventually had to throw it away. No antivirus software on the planet could save it. And the price of paying someone to clean out her hard drive was almost the same as buying a new computer. In the end, she opted for buying a new computer.

Frowning, Vienna clicked on the untitled email in her Spam folder. She squeezed her eyes shut as if a virus would spring out of the email and cause her computer to explode.

"As long as I don't download anything," she said to herself, "it should be okay. Looking never hurt anyone." Or at least she hoped not. She wasn't very computer literate. She only knew the basics and how to use certain software programs. She always felt that she knew just enough about computers to be dangerous.

Opening her eyes, she gasped.

"Vienna, please, I need to talk with you. It's important! Stop ignoring me. Jack"

Vienna had the sudden urge to slam her laptop closed. Her heart was pounding.

She wondered how he'd gotten her email. This was just too creepy.

She leapt up from the bed and ran over to the window. She parted two of the white wooden slats of her blinds and stared outside. Maybe she wasn't imagining being watched. Maybe someone really was out there. Vienna looked up and down the vacant street.

"Bunny," she said. She needed to talk to Bunny. If Bunny had given this guy Jack her number… But how would Bunny have gotten her phone number and email address? No, that didn't make sense. Bunny wouldn't have that information unless her father gave it to her, but she highly doubted it.

Vienna sat back down on the bed and stared at the open email. The whole thing was entirely too creepy. She shook her head while trying to come up with some sort of logical explanation for the text message and now the email.

The computer screen flickered.

"What the…?" Vienna reached for her mouse and

closed the email out. "This is crazy. What's going on with my computer? I should've never opened that email." The screen flickered again. Vienna slammed the laptop closed.

***

"Come on, Vienna," Jack hollered. "You've got to be the most stubborn…" He trailed off and spun up some energy to zap her computer causing the screen to flicker.

"Yes, that's right," he said, watching her expression. "It's me! I'm right here!" When Vienna didn't react, he manipulated the electricity in her computer and zapped the screen again. That's when Vienna slammed it shut.

Jack sighed. She was blocking out his voice again too. He wasn't quite sure what to do to break down her walls. Only she could do that. She was in control of her own body and mind. If only she'd stop being so narrow minded. He knew first hand that was not typical of her. Normally she was somewhat open for a human.

Jack paced back and forth across the bedroom wondering what to do next. He was contemplating using all of his energy that he could gather from the little bit of moisture in the night's air and materializing right now in her room. However, he was afraid that the combination of his full bodily appearance with Vienna's narrow mindedness would push her over the edge and land her in the loony bin. But maybe that's a chance that he'd need to take. Push her so close to the brink of insanity that she'd stop acting so childish and listen to what he had to say.

Jack focused on pushing energy into his fingertips. He conjured up just enough to part the blinds and look outside. He was curious as to what it was that Vienna had been looking at. He stared across the street and saw it, a dark silhouette in the shadows, by the street light. It was her. It had to be her. She was watching Vienna, waiting for her to fall asleep. That was when a human was most open to listening. The only problem was that most people chalked up their encounters as dreams or they didn't remember the encounter at all when they awoke.

Jack let the blinds fall shut with a clatter. Vienna looked up from the duffle bag she was rummaging through in search of her pajamas. He noticed the fear in her eyes. The fear was causing her to block him out. Instead of reacting, she grabbed her pajamas and entered the bathroom. Jack wasn't about to follow, he decided to give her a break. He'd come back and try to make contact with her later.

Saturday, May 14
Chapter 7

Vienna held the cherry by the stem and dunked it into her drink. She swirled it around and around. Glancing up from the little table, she stared at the empty stage. She then looked down at the petite rectangular face of her dainty gold watch. It was ten minutes 'til, almost time for the show to start. She looked up and noticed two men walking past her table. One of them, a tall stocky man with dark hair, turned around and grinned at her. She smiled then shyly glanced down at her drink and dunked the cherry again.

The two men sat down at a table near the bar. Vienna could barely see their faces because the lighting was so dim. They were talking and staring at her. The stocky man made eye contact and raised his glass as if in a toast. She could feel her cheeks reddening. Embarrassed at being caught staring back at him, she could barely lift her drink to toast him back because her hand was shaking. She shyly broke eye contact and took a sip.

More people filtered into the room and were being

seated at tables all around her. The chattering of the crowd and the laughter of the people at a table directly behind her became louder and louder as the club steadily filled up.

Vienna sipped at her drink, careful to keep her eyes focused on anything and everything that was not the two men. She could still feel their eyes watching her and couldn't shake that eerie feeling that pricked between her shoulder blades. Pushing aside the cherry in her glass to save for later, she pouted. She was a bit upset to see that her drink was mostly ice.

A waitress stopped by the table and set a Sex on the Beach in front of her. Vienna looked up at her, puzzled. Without saying a word, the waitress nodded in the direction of the two men. They had ordered her another drink. Vienna tried to see them through the now crowded room, but couldn't. She smiled and accepted the drink. Vienna snatched the cherry from her empty glass before the waitress took it away.

An older gentleman with a short round woman on his arm stopped by the table and asked if the other seats were taken.

"No," Vienna said, shaking her head. It was then that she realized her voice wasn't her own. She cleared her throat and took a gulp of her drink. It was bitter and a lot stronger than the other one. She cringed, and then tasted it again. Very bitter, she thought. It was then that she noticed the napkin beneath her drink. It had a phone number scribbled across it with a name. She glanced again in the direction of the bar, but still couldn't see the two men.

The lights dimmed even more and the stage lights

flashed on. A man dressed in drag, in a beautiful yellow gown and a body that most women would kill for, flounced onto the stage and began to sing, "I Will Survive."

The chattering audience quieted, enraptured by the show. Vienna glanced at the napkin. It was dark and she couldn't make out the name. She picked it up and caught sight of her nails. They were long, red, and acrylic. Since when did she have perfect nails? As an artist, she didn't wear fake nails. There wasn't any point to it. As soon as she pulled out her paints, they were thrashed.

"Great song, huh?" Sitting in the chair next to her was Jack. He was wearing a black, silk, button down shirt, dark blue jeans, and looked incredibly handsome. He flashed an award-winning smile.

She leaned in and hissed in his ear, "Where did you come from?"

"Just wanted to spend a little time with you. I like the new look," he said, ogling her short form-fitting red dress that matched her nails.

"What?" Vienna followed his stare to her dress and flinched.

A flash of red, she thought. What in the world was she wearing? Her eyes dropped self-consciously to the extreme shortness of her dress. She tugged at the hem to try to cover up her thighs. What could have possessed her to put something like this on? And in public? She didn't have the type of body to pull something like this off. At least she didn't think she did.

"I like it," Jack said.

Vienna let out an exasperated sigh and rolled her eyes. She took another sip of her drink.

"I'd go easy on that," Jack warned.

Vienna threw him a look. Who was he to tell her what to do and how much she could drink? Vienna put her head back and chugged down the rest of her Sex on the Beach just to spite him. She set the glass down on the table with a loud clink and smiled with satisfaction. All that was left was the cherry and ice.

There, she thought, take that!

He stopped smiling and shook his head.

The song ended and the audience applauded. Several people were giving standing ovations and cat calling. The curtains closed then reopened to show a Madonna look-a-like on stage. The music to the song Borderline began to play and the man in the yellow dress pranced on stage next to the man dressed like Madonna.

Vienna was having a hard time concentrating. The room was swaying back and forth. She was beginning to feel quite woozy.

Oh no, she thought as her stomach lurched into her chest, I'm going to throw up. I need some fresh air.

She grasped the edge of the table and stood up on wobbly legs. The room was spinning.

"Are you all right?" Jack asked. "Vienna?"

Vienna couldn't hear him. She couldn't hear anything in particular, just lots of loudness. Every sound was closing in on her in an incoherent mottled mess. She stumbled towards the door, tripping on her own feet and muttering apologies as she bumped into people's chairs.

Outside she bent over and heaved into the gutter. Through blurry vision, she recognized the street. She was on Palm Canyon drive in Palm Springs. It was the same street where the street fair was held on Thursday nights.

An arm encircled her waist. She looked at the man next to her. He was weaving in and out of her vision. She recognized him. She thought he must've been the one that sent her the drink.

"Vienna!" Jack shouted from the doorway of the bar. "Wake up! Vienna, wake up!"

The man urged Vienna to rest her head on his shoulder. She couldn't resist him even if she wanted to. She was so weak. He led her down the street and she let him.

"You don't have to do this," Jack said. He was now standing next to Vienna. "You've seen enough. Wake up!"

Vienna groggily leaned into the man. The top of her head was pressed into the crook of his neck. She knew she was walking, but how her legs were moving she wasn't sure. She couldn't feel them. It was almost as if she were floating. And her eyes were bugging her. Her vision kept blurring up. Everything was spinning out of control. She was afraid she was going to be sick again. She squeezed her eyes shut against the nausea.

Jack put his hand on Vienna's shoulder and began shaking her. "Wake up!" he demanded. "Don't do this to yourself! There's no need! Vienna, can you hear me? Wake up!"

Vienna muttered something incomprehensible. The next time she opened her eyes, she was in the alley. The same alley she'd passed out in during the street fair. But this was different. This wasn't her memory. This was something else entirely. Comprehension dawned on Vienna as she tried to make sense of what was happening. He had drugged her. Maybe that's what had happened to the girl in the alley. She tried to scream, but nothing happened. She couldn't open her mouth. She was paralyzed. The only screaming to be heard was within her own mind. Then she felt a sharp stabbing pain in her head. The pain was intolerable.

"Vienna," Jack said, standing next to her bed and shaking her shoulder. "Wake up! You're dreaming. Vienna!" He'd conjured up his energy and was in physical form.

"What?" Vienna sat straight up, eyes open wide. "Oh!" She placed her hands to her heart. "What are you doing here?" she shrieked, grabbing the comforter and pulling it up to her chin.

"It's okay," he said, laying his hand on her shoulder, trying to comfort her. "You're okay now."

Vienna grabbed his hand and flung it away from her. She scooted her body as far back as she could with her back pressed against the headboard.

"No, it's not okay! What are you doing in my room? How'd you get in here?"

Jack took a couple of steps back and sat at the foot of the bed. "It's difficult to explain."

"It was Bunny," Vienna gasped, tugging again at the comforter, using it as a protective barrier between her and Jack. "That's how you know things. You know, like my phone number and stuff."

"What? Bunny? No."

"She let you in here," Vienna spat. "I knew it!" She tossed the comforter and jumped out of bed. "I'm going to give her a piece of my mind! How dare she!"

"No, Vienna, wait," Jack stood up, "let me explain. This has nothing to do with Bunny."

Vienna was already in the hallway and heading for her father's bedroom. The thought of Bunny sleeping in her father's bed made her even more furious. She grabbed the doorknob and flung the bedroom door open. "Bunny!"

"Huh?" Bunny was lying in bed. The drapes were still drawn and the room was semi-dark. She had a beige satin sleeping mask over her eyes. "Vienna?" She slid the mask up and blinked hard and sleepily while propping herself up on one elbow. "What's wrong?"

Vienna stared at Bunny's bloodshot, swollen eyes. She looked as if she'd been up crying all night. There's no way she'd been up early this morning orchestrating a plan to get Vienna and Jack together. It was obvious she'd been sound asleep when Vienna entered. Feeling a bit odd, and confused, Vienna asked, "Um, do you know anyone named Jack?"

"Jack?" Bunny seemed puzzled. "Jack who?"

"About this tall," Vienna said, holding her hand up above her head. "Light brown hair and blue eyes…"

"I don't think so," Bunny said. "Why? What's wrong? What happened?"

"Oh," Vienna said, not sure how to explain. "It's nothing. Just thought you might know him. I'll let you go back to sleep. Sorry I bothered you." Quietly she backed out of the bedroom and shut the door behind her.

She returned to her room to find it empty. There was no sign of Jack. Not even a sign that he had been there. She couldn't help but wonder if she dreamt the entire thing.

"This is ridiculous," she mumbled, shaking her head and stepping into the bathroom. "I swear I'm losing my mind."

Vienna turned on the tap in the shower to warm the water. A hot shower would help to wake her up and clear her mind. Dangling her fingers in the running water, feeling the temperature gradually change from cold to warm, she thought about Jack and all the weird things going on.

The conclusion she came up with was that she was losing her mind. And coming to the desert was playing into her crazy delusions. Chasing a stupid reoccurring nightmare was doing nothing but wasting her time and causing her dreams to feel like reality. She needed to put an end to things before they got completely out of control. As of right now, nothing was making any sense.

Last night's dream lingered at the back of her mind. But she kept it there, refusing to think any more about it. It had felt so real and scary that it was unnerving. She didn't ever want to have a bad dream like that again.

"You're not losing your mind," whispered a man's voice in her right ear. It was deep and hollow and she could feel breath on her neck.

Vienna stood up and spun around. No one was there. The bathroom was empty. Her eyes were drawn to a small amount of steam settling on the mirror above the sink. The words HELP ME were no longer there. Bunny had to have wiped down the mirror since then.

"Who said that?" she asked once she found her voice.

"Me." Steam swirled and collected in the air, swarming together, forming a sphere. Within moments, the steam darkened and solidified into the shape of a human.

Vienna blinked. Jack was standing in front of her with his back to the mirror. He smiled warmly at Vienna.

"Ta da," Jack said, arms outstretched as if he'd just performed a really cool magic trick and was waiting for applause.

Vienna just stood there. She didn't know if she should scream or faint. Both would be appropriate. But instead, she did neither. She stumbled over to the toilet and sat on the fuzzy pink lid. She leaned her head against the wall to let the wanting to faint, pass.

"Well," Jack said. "What do you think?"

Vienna lifted her head. "What do I think?" she asked, feeling her strength returning. "How the...? I mean, what in the...? Okay. I, uh..." She couldn't think of anything. Her mind was blank. "This is crazy. I mean..."

"Don't say anything," Jack said, holding his index finger up, silencing her.

Vienna opened her mouth to protest, but then stopped. She nodded instead. It was best to let him explain what was going on because she had no clue what had just happened.

Well, she wouldn't say she had no clue. She did have a clue. A man somehow appeared out of nowhere. She saw it with her own eyes. He wasn't there, and then he was. She had no idea how he did it. There was no logical explanation for his appearance.

"Okay, here it goes. The explanation you've been waiting for," he said, breaking the silence. "I'm your spirit guide."

Vienna waited for him to continue, but he didn't. He just stood there grinning at her as if that explained everything.

"My what?"

"Your... spirit... guide," he repeated, slowly as if

saying the words slower and more clearly would clarify everything.

"And...?" she prompted, when she realized he wasn't about to explain further.

"That's about it," he said, shrugging. "That's why I'm here."

Vienna made a face. "I don't get it."

"I'm your spirit guide," Jack repeated, looking a bit confused.

"Yeah, okay," she said. "I don't believe in spirit guides. However, let's say you are one of those guides. So, why are you here?"

"I'm your guide. And I'm here to help you. We made a pact before you came here."

"Before I came to the desert?" Vienna rubbed her temples. She felt a stress headache coming on. "I don't..."

"No," he chuckled, "before you came to earth."

It was Vienna's turn to laugh. What Jack was implying sounded completely absurd.

"That's crazy! You mean before I was born?" she asked, snidely. "You and I made some sort of deal when I was an itsy bitsy baby?"

Jack didn't notice the sarcasm. His train of thought was too literal for that. "You weren't a baby before you came here," he said, shaking his head. "You do not understand. I'm not choosing the correct words to explain." He took in a deep breath then released. "Yes, I guess you can look at it as a deal."

"This is totally nuts," she said while getting up from the toilet. "I'm dreaming. This isn't real. You're not real."

"This is real." Jack held his hand up to touch Vienna's cheek. "I'm real." She flinched and backed away before he could touch her. "I'm here to help you. I'm using all of my energy to be in this form," he said, softly. "Please. I don't have much time before it fades."

He tried again to brush Vienna's cheek with his fingers. This time she didn't back away. She let him. His fingertips gently brushed her skin. They were cold, but soft. She looked into his blue eyes. Not another word was spoken. Tingles of electricity enveloped her body. Closing her eyes, she enjoyed the sensation. When she reopened them, he was gone.

***

After a shower and a bowl of cereal, Vienna laid on her stomach across her bed and Googled *Spirit Guides* on her laptop. She found hundreds to thousands of websites and so much contradicting information that she wasn't sure what the true facts were.

Again, she found herself staring at Wikipedia and the simple definition it gave for a spirit guide.

Spirit guide is a term used by the Western tradition of Spiritualist Churches, mediums, and psychics to describe an entity that remains a disincarnate spirit in order to act as a guide or protector to a living incarnated human being.

Traditionally, within the spiritualist churches, spirit guides were often stereotyped ethnically, with Native Americans, Chinese or Egyptians being popular for their perceived ancient wisdom. Other popular types of guides were saints or other enlightened individuals. Nevertheless, the term can also refer to totems, angels, guardian angels or nature spirits.

Vienna read this passage several times and wasn't quite sure how she felt about it. She'd never really given psychics or mediums a second thought. To her they were right up there with werewolves, vampires and ghosts. They didn't exist. They were chalked up with fairytales and children stories. But now she wasn't so sure.

"This is stupid," she said, still staring at the screen.

"Knock, knock," Bunny called, opening the door. "You've been in here all morning." She glimpsed the laptop on the bed. "Oh, are you doing homework?"

"Uh, no," Vienna said, closing the laptop, but not before Bunny got a look at the screen.

"Spirit guides?" Bunny asked, her beautiful turquoise eyes growing wide. "I didn't know you were a believer."

"Well, I'm..."

"I know this woman who gives fantastic readings," Bunny said, her eyes still bulging. "She said my spirit guide's name is Priscilla."

"You believe in spirit guides?" Vienna asked.

"Of course," Bunny gushed, clutching her hands in front of her chest and tilting her head to the side. "I believe in everything spiritual. Oh, this is so nice to have someone to talk to about this. You know, your father sees everything black and white. It's either this way or that way and that's it. He has tunnel vision. So I can't talk about this kind of stuff with him. When I do, he just kind of humors me. This is so fantastic! We have so much in common!"

"Oh," Vienna said, sitting upright. "I'm just..."

"I have some books you can borrow," she said. "Do you believe in ghosts, too? I have this great book on spirits, ghosts, and angels."

"You believe in ghosts?"

"Oh, yes," Bunny said. "They fascinate me. Those poor lost souls trapped in between. I wish I could help them."

"What do you mean by trapped?"

"You know, when they die they don't go to the other side. Sometimes they're angry about things, or they're scared. It could be all sorts of things. Some people just don't want to give up their life or just don't want to leave so they stay here."

"Do they ever get lost?" Vienna asked.

"In a way, I think all ghosts are lost. And I think that sometimes they don't even realize they're dead. They just sorta keep living their lives in their mind. Kinda like a time warp."

"Wow," Vienna said. "You really know a lot about ghosts. Have you ever seen one?"

"I wish," Bunny said. "It's just not my gift, I guess. I have a blind faith. I know they're there and I believe, but I can't see them to help them."

"I don't know what I believe," Vienna said. "I'm confused."

"It's good to have an open mind," Bunny said.

"Just out of curiosity, how would someone help a ghost?"

Bunny shrugged. "Depends on what's keeping them here."

"I don't know," Vienna said, shaking her head. "It all seems so fanciful. And spirit guides, I'm not too sure about what they do. It's all a little much for me."

"Oh," Bunny looked excited, "I have a book on how

to contact your spirit guide if you'd like to read it. It might help with some of your questions. I've tried numerous times to contact my guide, but I just can't seem to communicate with Priscilla. Not in the way I'd like to, anyway. I'll be right back." She vanished from the room in search of her books.

"Getting in contact with my spirit guide isn't the problem," Vienna muttered beneath her breath. "It's getting me to believe I have one."

For a split second, Vienna felt a little more at ease with the explanation that Jack had given her for his appearance. Bunny's belief in spirit guides seemed to ease her mind a bit. She wondered just how much information she should reveal to Bunny. The last thing she wanted was this to get back to her family. They weren't believers and she knew they'd think she was nuts.

Chapter 8

Vienna peered into her rearview mirror and squinted against the bright headlights of the car behind her. She was slowly driving down Palm Canyon drive in search of the club from her dream last night. She wished she knew the name. All she knew was that it had to be near the alley where the girl in her dream had been killed.

A horn blared as the car behind her impatiently flashed its headlights and zipped into the right lane, speeding around her.

"Sorry," Vienna muttered, waving sheepishly. She knew she was driving at a snail's pace, but she didn't want to accidentally pass the club. Being that Palm Canyon was a one way street, she'd have to go down one of the side streets and around the block if she passed it. She didn't want to do the circuit again since this was her second time down the strip already. And for some reason, she seemed to be hitting all of the red lights.

Inching along, Vienna examined the shops, restaurants, and bars on the left side of the street. Her gut told her it was on the left side, not the right. She tried to remember exactly what she saw when she stumbled out of the club in her dream. However, her visions were so hazy and everything was dark. It was hard to remember.

Vienna reached for the knob on the stereo and turned down the music to help with her concentration. She'd spent the day researching Bunny's books and listening to her nonstop chattering about the paranormal. Even though Bunny went on and on and a couple of times she just wanted to tell the woman to leave her alone, she had to admit, Bunny knew a lot of interesting things. Whether or not they were true, she didn't know. She still was having a hard time believing anything about the paranormal; spirit guides, psychics, ghosts, etc. But she was trying to keep an open mind.

Somehow, she had managed to ask Bunny all sorts of questions without spilling the beans about her having a handsome spirit guide named Jack, following her around, appearing in planes, at street fairs, in dreams, bedrooms, and bathrooms and without having to mention her other crazy dreams that had spurred this unplanned visit to the desert to begin with.

"Here," she said, "this is it." Vienna pulled up and carefully backed in her rental car, parallel parking against the curb.

She glanced out the window. There was a painted rust colored cement bench with a man and woman sitting together, talking. In front of them was a tourist shop with T-shirts on display in the window. She didn't remember seeing the gift shop or any other shops in her dream.

Shrugging, Vienna decided to go with her gut feeling. She grabbed her purse and hopped out of the car. She stared at the tourist shop for a moment and then decided to go for a little stroll. She followed the sidewalk while gazing at the shops. Tourists and young couples in search of something to do on a Saturday night, filled the shops, and wandered the sidewalks. Music floated on the warm night air. Vienna could hear laughing, talking, and the scent of Mexican food taunted her as she walked past an outdoor restaurant. Through an iron fence, she could see a live band playing and people were drinking and dancing.

Vienna kept walking. She walked past a frozen yogurt shop and another outdoor restaurant. She passed the pub where she met up with Bunny the night of the street fair. She continued to walk and the streets became silent and dark. She was no longer on the strip. She was heading in the direction of the alley with the dumpster. But before she reached the alley, she felt compelled to stop. She could hear muffled music and singing. She backtracked a few steps and stopped in front of a solid wood door. There were no windows. She could barely hear the music coming from inside. Suddenly, her stomach lurched.

This had to be it. She knew it by the sudden wave of nausea that came out of nowhere. Closing her eyes and forcing herself to calm her nerves, she reached for the door handle.

"Okay," she whispered. "Here goes nothing."

The door wouldn't budge. She tried shaking the twisted metal handle.

Nothing. It was locked.

Okay, now what? she wondered.

Feeling frustrated, she shook the handle harder. The murmur of music could still be heard through the door. She knew someone was inside.

Putting her face as close to the door as possible she

called, "Hello! Hello?"

Nothing happened. That wasn't going to work.

Vienna frowned and regrouped her thoughts. She started knocking on the door. Her knocks sounded faint on the heavy wood, so she took it up a notch. She knocked harder and harder until her knocks became a desperate loud pounding.

Suddenly the door flew open. Vienna stood with fist still in midair. She'd been making such a racket at the door that she hadn't even heard the music stop. A very ticked off black man in a yellow miniskirt and white halter-top, glared at her. He had one hand on his hip. The other hip was jutting out to the right. He tapped the toe of a golden stiletto on the floor in aggravation.

"I, um," Vienna began.

"This better be important," he spat, batting his false lashes at her. "You interrupted my practicing. We don't open for another hour."

Vienna stared at his bright yellow eye shadow and silver sparkling eyeliner. She recognized him. He was the guy dressed in drag, handing out flyers at the street fair. She also saw him in her dream. She was positive it was him that was performing.

"Well?" he asked. "What do you want?""

When she didn't answer quickly enough, he began to close the door.

"Wait!" Vienna screamed, jamming her shoulder in the door so he couldn't close it.

"Girl," he said, "I told you we don't open for an hour. What's gone and got your panties in a twist?"

"I need to talk to you," she said.

He shook his head. "I've no time. Gotta get my wig

on." He patted the back of his head, flashing sparkling yellow acrylic nails.

"It's important."

"Talk to me after the show. Like I said, I ain't got no time."

"Please," Vienna begged, refusing to move out of the way.

"Ralph!" the man screeched over his shoulder. A large burly Hispanic man with a salt and pepper beard, black T-shirt stretched over a protruding beer belly, and sunglasses came to the door. "Get rid of her. I need to primp."

"Wait!" Vienna cried.

"Vienna," a familiar voice said over her right shoulder.

Vienna turned her head to see Jack standing behind her. Instead of feeling shocked by his appearance, she actually felt quite relieved.

"Jack," she said, her body still wedged in the doorway.

"Sorry, Miss," the bouncer said in a low voice. "You'll have to leave."

"Is there any way she could just ask a few harmless questions?" Jack intervened.

"Come back in an hour," the bouncer said, gently removing Vienna from the doorway. "That's when the show starts."

The man in the yellow miniskirt heard Jack's voice and peeked over the bouncer's shoulder to get a look at the other visitor.

"Why my heavens," he gasped, shoving himself in-between the bodyguard and Vienna. "Who is this vision of hunkiness?"

"I'm Jack," Jack said, "I'm Vienna's..."

"Friend," she said, quickly. The last thing she needed was for Jack to announce that he was her spirit guide.

"Just a friend?" the man asked, batting his lashes.

"Yes," Vienna said. "Just a friend."

"Well, why didn't you tell me you had such a hottie with you?" The man put his hand on the bouncer's shoulder and gently squeezed. "It's okay, Ralph. Let them in. They're with me."

Ralph stepped aside and let both Vienna and Jack enter the club. He stepped outside, peered up and down the street then came back in and shut the door behind him.

"You can help me with my hair." The man in the yellow mini skirt clutched hold of Jack's arm. He ran his fingers over his biceps. "Such big muscles. Do you work out?"

"No."

"You can call me Jamie. Or if you'd rather call me by my stage name, Goldie, that'll be just fine. In fact, you can call me whatever you want."

"Goldie," Jack said, very seriously. "Vienna has a few questions to ask you."

Goldie looked Vienna up and down. "All right, watcha want?"

"There was this girl that came to hear you sing. She had dark hair and was about my height. I need information about her."

"Okay, shoot. When was this?" Goldie asked, staring up at Jack.

Jack nodded at Vienna to continue.

"Um," she frowned. "I'm not sure. But she was in a red dress… Really pretty… And left with a man."

"Well, that narrows it down," Goldie said, sarcastically. "Honey, that describes just about every other woman at my club."

"She was drugged up, stumbling. I think something was put in her drink."

"In my club? Nuh-uh. Nothing like that happens here. I run a clean establishment. Just ask anybody. And I refuse to have you trashin' my place. I don't like your accusations." Goldie let go of Jack's arm and gave him a once over. "I ain't got time for this. You're cute, but not that cute."

"Wait, please," Vienna said. "You must remember her. She's in trouble."

"What sort of trouble?" Goldie asked. Vienna thought she heard a hint of concern in his voice.

"She's been murdered," Jack said.

Goldie gasped dramatically and put his long slender fingers over his lips. "I can't believe it. How do you know? You cops?"

Jack looked at Vienna.

Vienna shook her head.

He nodded again, urging her to explain.

"Fine," she said to Jack and turned her attention to Goldie. "This is going to sound ridiculous, but here goes nothing." Vienna took in a deep breath then said, "She's in my dreams. I've seen it happen."

Vienna could feel her face flush as Goldie gasped again. However, his reaction to what she told him wasn't what she had expected.

Goldie clutched hold of Vienna's hand. "Girl, why

didn't you just tell me you were psychic?"

"I, uh, I wouldn't call it that…"

"Vienna, draw a picture of the girl," Jack prompted.

"You can do that?" Goldie asked.

"Yeah, um, I'll try. People aren't really my thing. They look more animated than real." Vienna dug into her purse and found a black ballpoint pen and her paperwork for the rental car. She set the paperwork down on a table and began to sketch the girl on the backside of it.

"Goooldieee," called a man made up as Marilyn Monroe. He stepped out from behind the curtains on the stage. "I need some lip liner. Can I borrow yours?"

"Go ahead," Goldie said, flashing his yellow nails. "I don't know if I have your color though."

Marilyn disappeared behind stage.

"He's always forgettin' something," Goldie spat. "First it's mascara, then its hairspray, and now it's lip liner. I swear he'd lose his head if it weren't attached."

Vienna raised her eyebrows then went back to the sketch. She could hear clinking of glasses from the other end of the room as the two bartenders and the wait-staff prepared for the club to open.

Goldie peered over Vienna's shoulder, making her feel nervous as she tried to remember how the woman from her dreams looked. She darkened the hair and embellished the eyes. Vienna remembered her eyes being dark and soulful. Almost like a puppy giving you the sad eyes while begging for another treat.

"I know her," Goldie sang, excitedly. "I remember her clear as day."

"You do?" Vienna felt proud of her artistic skills. Maybe getting an art degree wasn't a waste after all. She glanced over at Jack who smiled at her.

"Yes," he seethed, suddenly changing his attitude. He jutted out his bottom lip and planted his hands on his hips. "She made me so mad. She, in her slinky little red dress and fabulous curves, got up right in the middle of a performance and left. All eyes were on her. Completely ruined my show. Almost made me forget my lines. I was singing a duet with Madonna, you know."

"Who was she with?"

"Madonna? She was with me. We were on stage."

"No. Not Madonna, the girl in red. Was she with anyone?"

Goldie sighed and his broad shoulders relaxed. "You say she's dead?"

Vienna nodded. "I think so."

Goldie shook his head. "She was with a man, like you said. He walked her out."

"Do you know him?"

Goldie chewed on his thick lower lip. "He's sort of a regular. Comes in from time to time. Sometimes with a friend. Sometimes alone. I don't think I've seen him in a while, though. In fact, come to think of it, I don't think he's been in since that night."

"Would you be able to point him out to us?" Jack asked. "If he were to come in?"

Goldie mulled this over for a moment. "This ain't no good for my business, you know."

"He murdered someone," Jack reminded.

Goldie huffed and crossed his freshly waxed arms over his broad chest. "Fine. I'll do what I can. Right now, I need to get ready. I need to stuff my bra and put on my wig. If I see him, or that friend he's been with, I'll point them out. You owe me one." He wagged a long finger at Vienna. "I want a free reading or somethin'. Maybe you could get in touch with my granny." With a flash of glittering yellow nails, he glided gracefully from the room.

***

The room filled up with chattering people. Vienna and Jack sat at the same table she had seen the girl sit at in her dreams. She found it kind of eerie. Vienna tried hard not to think of it, but how could she not.

"I'm going to have to leave soon," Jack whispered.

"What?" Vienna's stomach lurched at the thought. "What do you mean you have to leave soon?"

"I don't have enough energy to hold this form," Jack explained. "I've got to go."

"You can't leave me," Vienna whispered, harshly. "I thought you're here to help me?"

"I am." Jack looked around. "I'm always here."

"Wait," Vienna said as Jack got up from the table. "Don't go." He ignored her and briskly headed for the back of the room to avoid being watched as he vanished.

Suddenly frightened at the possibility of being at Goldie's alone, Vienna hopped up from the table and tried to follow him. She wasn't brave enough to do this on her own. Heck, she didn't even know what it was she was supposed to do. She wasn't a cop. She had no detective skills. And she had no proof that a supposed guy, she didn't even know, murdered a girl in a red dress that had appeared in her dream. What in the world was she supposed to do with that information, anyway? She was an artist for goodness sake, not a detective.

"Jack!" she whispered, chasing after him, trying to get

83

him to stop. "Jack!"

Jack didn't turn around. He continued towards the restrooms that were in a hallway to the left of the bar. Vienna pushed between two people that stepped in front of her. When she reached out to touch Jack's shoulder, he was gone. In fact, she didn't even see him vanish. He was there one moment, and then she blinked, and poof, no more Jack.

"Great," she groaned, "Houdini's done it again." Just then the door to the men's restroom swung open and almost hit her. Vienna jumped out of the way.

"Sorry," said a man, an inch or so taller than her with dark messy hair and a thick five o'clock shadow. He scratched at his scruffy chin.

"It's okay," Vienna said, not giving him a second glance. She headed back to her table. There were two men sitting there.

"I'm sorry were you sitting here?" asked one of the men. He was sitting in Jack's seat. He was a middle-aged gentleman with premature graying hair, a snow-white mustache and neatly trimmed beard.

Vienna lifted her purse that she'd accidentally left on her chair when she had dashed after Jack. "No, my friend had to leave. So, it's all yours." She pulled the chair out to retake her seat. "The other seats aren't taken either."

"Oh, good," the man said. "We were afraid we wouldn't get good seats. I'm Max, by the way, and this is William."

William had blonde hair, blue eyes and a baby face. Both men were probably around the same age, but William looked ten to fifteen years younger. He was seated next to Max, casually leaning back in his chair, sipping on a beer.

He nodded in response to the introduction.

"Hi, I'm Vienna," she said, shaking Max's hand and then reaching over the table to shake William's hand.

"This is our first time to Palm Springs," Max said. "We're taking a mini vacation. I heard that this show is really something."

Vienna smiled, politely. "That's what I've heard, too. So where are you from?"

"We live in Orange County. We drove out for a golf tournament and decided to stay a few days before returning home."

Vienna nodded, but was having a hard time concentrating on what Max was telling her. She heard something about Orange County, but the rest wasn't processing. Her thoughts had drifted elsewhere. From behind, she felt like she was being watched. Flashes from her nightmare were plaguing her. She had the same sensation from the dream that the girl did. A man was watching her from over near the bar. She knew it because of a weird tingling sensation in between her shoulder blades.

Looking over her shoulder, she studied the men and women sitting at tables near the bar at the other end of the room. The lights had just dimmed and she was having a hard time making out faces. From what she could tell, even in the dim room, no one in particular was taking any interest in her. She chalked up her uncomfortable feelings to her overactive imagination. She wished Jack was there. He'd make her feel a little less on edge.

Vienna lifted her diet soda to her lips and sipped. Before Jack had done his little disappearing act on her, she'd ordered something to drink and had totally forgotten all about it. The waitress had delivered her soda while she had been chasing Jack down. She was still pretty ticked off about him leaving her like this.

What kind of spirit guide was he anyway? she wondered.

Vienna ran her finger down the side of the cold glass making a line in the condensation. She'd purposely ordered something nonalcoholic to avoid having an episode like what had happened to the girl in her dream. Even though she knew that it wasn't the girl's fault if something had been put in her drink. But she still wanted to do what she could to make sure she had her wits about her. A clear head is what she needed right now.

"Guess it's going to start soon," Max said. "We heard that Goldie is fabulous!"

"Me, too," Vienna said, leaning back in her chair. "He's quite dramatic."

The stage lights came on and Goldie pranced out onto the stage in four-inch heels. Immediately the audience began to applaud. Goldie broke out into song and the room quieted.

Vienna tried to concentrate on Goldie, but couldn't shake the eerie feeling of being watched. A gust of cold air blasted the side of her face and chilled her to the bone. Hairs on the back of her neck stood on end.

Why was it getting so cold? she wondered.

Vienna coughed and swore she saw her breath before she covered her mouth. She looked over to see Max rub the palms of her hands over her arms. She surmised that she wasn't the only one feeling cold. But William sitting on the other side of Max seemed fine. The cold air seemed to be concentrated around her.

Looking up towards the ceiling, Vienna expected to

see an air-conditioning vent. The ceiling was high and dark so she couldn't see anything. And if there was a vent, it was pretty high up there.

Another wave of chills came over her. This time an icy stream of air tickled her ear from behind as if someone was blowing on it. Turning her head, Vienna glanced at the table of people seated there. None of them seemed in the least bit chilly. Their eyes were glued to Goldie.

Vienna looked beyond them and saw a woman in a red dress, long dark hair, and pale skin, standing by the bar. The woman was facing the bar as if waiting for the bartender. She turned her head in Vienna's direction and for a second, they made eye contact. The young woman's blackened eyes startled her. When Vienna blinked, she was gone.

Was it the same girl from her dream? It happened so fast. Maybe she was just imagining her. She hated doubting herself, but she couldn't help it. She shouldn't be seeing dead people. It was just too weird.

Vienna blinked again, hard. The young woman didn't reappear, but she noticed a man seated at a table near the bar. He was staring at her. He was the scruffy looking man that almost hit her with the bathroom door.

Is that who's making me feel uneasy? she wondered. *Maybe the girl in the red dress wanted me to see him.*

Turning back around, Vienna slumped down in her seat and tried to pay attention to the show. Goldie had just finished his song and was announcing the next act. Vienna wasn't sure what she was supposed to do next. She hoped it would just come to her if she waited patiently. Unfortunately, patience wasn't something that came easy for her. She picked up her soda and took a long sip.

When the show ended, Vienna was still at a loss as to what she should be doing. And Jack had never returned to help her. She felt both odd and out of place sitting at the table without a date or a friend or something.

The overhead lights turned on and people were chattering noisily to each other. Vienna said her goodbyes to Max and William and wished them a happy stay in Palm Springs. When they were gone, she made a b-line for the little girl's room. Her bladder was about to explode after drinking two large sodas. She raced to the restroom, dodging people left and right, and was relieved to find no line. How often did that happen in a woman's restroom?

Once finished, she washed her hands, and stared at her reflection in the mirror. She knew she was looking at herself, but she seemed different somehow. Not that her outer appearance was different. She still had the same dark brown unruly hair that had a mind of its own, rounded face with slight cheekbones, a nose she felt was too large for her face, and pretty enough hazel brown eyes. But there was a different feel about her.

So many changes were taking place on the inside. It was as if a dormant part of her soul was awakening. A part of her she never knew existed. She was no longer just an art student. She was something more. What she was, she wasn't quite sure. Her life was now complicated since Jack's arrival.

It was hard for her to believe in spirit guides and ghosts. Her parents weren't believers of the spiritual realm and this was against everything she'd been taught. And it was completely against the social norms.

Vienna dried her hands and decided that her next step

would be to talk to Goldie. Flinging open the door, Vienna stepped into the hall that housed the restrooms. A man was leaning against the wall as if he was waiting for someone. He was the same man that had been staring at her, the same man that almost hit her with the bathroom door earlier. However, he wasn't the man that she'd seen in her dreams. He was shorter, somewhat wiry, and not as attractive.

"Hey," he said, upon noticing Vienna.

Vienna nodded and flashed a shy smile. "Hi."

"Sorry about almost slamming you with the door earlier."

"No problem," Vienna said. She started to walk away when she felt his warm hand on her forearm, stopping her.

"You here alone?" he asked, his intense green eyes met hers.

"Umm…" Vienna wasn't quite sure what to say. Should she say yes or no? Saying yes might open up the door to ask him questions. He might be the friend of the guy from her dream. Quickly she decided on a safe answer. "Yes. I came with a friend, but he had to leave."

"Oh," he said, his hand still clutching her arm. "Can I walk you to your car? Maybe get your number?"

"Oh. Um, no, that's okay. He should be back soon. My friend, that is," Vienna added, releasing her arm from his grasp. "He only had to leave for a little bit." She felt that if he knew she had a male friend returning at any moment, he'd be a little more hesitant if he were dangerous and wishing to do her harm.

"I see," he said, with a curt nod. He scratched at his messy hair. "Sorry to bother you."

"Vienna, honey!" Goldie glided through the crowd

of people that were either finishing their drinks before the club closed their doors or getting up from their tables to leave. "It's so nice of you to come!" He grabbed hold of Vienna's shoulders and planted a kiss on each cheek, leaving a set of glittering gold lips. "And who is this young man with you?"

"Umm… we just met."

"I've seen you before. You sometimes come in with a friend," Goldie said, wagging a finger at him. "What's your name, honey?"

"Ryan," he said, shyly. His eyes darted to the door.

"Ryan," Goldie said, flashing his nails in the air. "Are you givin' my girl here a hard time?"

"Uh, no."

"No worries. I'm only jokin'. So, who's the cutie, the one with the dark wavy hair that's usually with you? Big guy, about yay tall…" Goldie fluttered his false lashes and held his hand up in the air. "Come on, don't be shy with little old Goldie. I don't bite, honey. Tell me his name. He's a real cutie pie."

"Nathan," Ryan said, then cleared his throat.

"Nathan," Goldie repeated. He winked at Vienna. "And where is this Nathan? Why's he missin' my show? I haven't seen him in at least a couple weeks now."

"I, uh," Ryan uttered. Vienna could tell he felt put on the spot to give an answer. "I haven't seen him. We, uh, we work together and he hasn't been in. It's not as if we hang out or anything. We just come here for the cheap beers after work sometimes."

Goldie spat, his voice dropping an octave, "I know it ain't just for the beers. It's the music, too."

Vienna cringed at the unexpected voice change.

90

Goldie was really ticked off at the thought of two of his regular customers frequenting his club only for the cheap beer. Regaining his composure, he cleared his throat and smiled a really big exaggerated smile.

"What a shame your friend isn't here," Goldie said, his voice soft, batting his lashes again. "Is he sick? A cutie like that should never be too sick to come see my show. I know he didn't just come for the beer. He appreciated my talent, unlike some people."

"I, uh, I think he quit or something. Probably moved. I don't know." Ryan shrugged. He eyed the front door again. It was obvious he felt uncomfortable and wanted to dart from the room. "I need to get going." When he went to leave, Goldie stepped in front of him, cornering him.

"Where do you work?" Goldie asked, hands firmly planted on his snake hips. He jutted one out to the side.

"What? Where I work? Why?"

"Just curious." Goldie stood in front of him, twirling a wavy lock of fake hair, waiting for an answer.

"I install computers for people and fix them and stuff."

"Do you do house calls?"

"I really should be…"

"Do you drive one of them computer bug cars with the cute little antennae?" Goldie asked, holding his index fingers up to his head, mimicking an insect. "I love those little green bugs. Have you seen those, Vienna? They're so cute!"

Vienna nodded. "Yeah, they are cute." She'd seen those funny green cars several times before while visiting the desert. She remembered one in particular that had googly eyes attached to the antennae.

"Uh, yeah, well, the cars are company owned. A kind of advertisement," he said. "I really gotta go. Uh, nice meeting you, Vienna."

"Nice meeting you, too," Vienna said.

Goldie stepped aside and Ryan escaped the club in a flash. Vienna had never seen anyone move so fast before. Well, not counting Jack. That was different. He wasn't quite human. Vienna had noticed that Goldie's questioning seemed to make Ryan uneasy and she wasn't quite sure why. It could be that he was just shy, which she doubted because of the way he had grabbed her arm to ask her out. He was pretty forward about meeting her. Or it could've been that Goldie made him feel nervous, which she could understand. Goldie had a very big presence full of strong, overbearing energy. But then again, who knows? Maybe it wasn't either of those things. It was hard to tell.

Goldie leaned in and whispered in Vienna's ear, "You owe me one, sweet cheeks."

***

Vienna waited until the club was empty before walking out to her car. Goldie had disappeared behind stage to change along with the other singers and dancers. Wait staff and bouncers did their duties, shuffling around the almost empty building.

After waiting for what seemed to be an eternity for Jack to return, but what was in reality about twenty minutes, Vienna got tired of waiting and stepped out into the dry, chilly, yet not too chilly, desert night. She walked briskly down the dark sidewalk. She headed for her car that was parked along the street.

The souvenir T-shirt store that she had parked in front of was closed with all lights turned off except a security lamp. The streets for the most part were vacant. The faint sound of music floated on the air from the local pub on the corner.

Vienna already had her car keys in hand. She looked up and down the street and unlocked the driver's side door. She glanced in the backseat just to be on the safe side, saw that it was empty, and hopped in. Locking the door behind her, she felt a little more at ease.

The guy, Ryan, at the club had made her feel anxious. For some reason, he really creeped her out. But then again, he was the friend, or co-worker, to the guy that was the murderer in her dream. That was probably enough reason to creep anyone out.

"I can't believe this is happening to me," Vienna said, staring at her eyes in the rearview mirror. She was more than grateful to see that they were her eyes staring back and not someone else's. "I still don't know if any of this is even real."

Starting up her car, she pulled out onto the street and headed down Palm Canyon when she noticed that something was flapping beneath her windshield wiper. It was a yellow piece of paper.

"Ugh, I hate those." Putting on her blinker, she pulled over and got out of the car to remove the flyer. Vienna unfolded the flyer as she plopped back into the driver's seat. It was an advertisement for Goldie's Club. Across the middle, a name and phone number was printed in bold black marker.

Call me! Ryan 760-444-3242

Vienna sucked in air and set the note on the

passenger seat. "See what happens when you leave me in the lurch?" she said aloud, hoping that Jack could hear her. "Men ask me out."

She switched on the stereo and turned up the tunes. The song Bullet Proof was playing. She loved that song, and began to sing along. That's when it struck her. How did Ryan know which car was hers? He left the club before she did. Did he see her arrive? She figured he had to have. There was no other explanation. But she had arrived at least an hour or so before the club had even opened. Maybe he had been sitting outside somewhere waiting to get in. She tried to remember if she'd seen him and searched her memory. She could only remember seeing a guy and girl sitting on the bench where she parked. But then again, at the time, it wasn't as if she was looking for anyone in particular. Her mind was preoccupied on finding the club from her dream. For all she knew, Ryan could've been walking behind her then watching her bang on the door of Goldie's.

"That's creepy," she said, fighting the chills that crawled all over her flesh. She realized that he had to have been watching her when she walked up the street to the club. She couldn't think of any other explanation.

"Are you going to call him?" asked a disembodied voice from the back seat.

Startled, Vienna swerved her car and quickly jerked it back into her lane. "What the...! You scared me! Don't ever do that again, you hear me!" She turned down the music and glanced in the rearview mirror. "Where are you?"

"I'm here," Jack said.

"Why can't I see you?" Vienna quickly glanced over

her shoulder in case it was just too dark to see him in the mirror. No one was there.

"I don't have enough energy to manifest physically. You can see me if you want to. You have the gift. Just open your mind."

"This is too weird," Vienna said. "I don't know what to think anymore."

"You'll learn to control your abilities. It takes patience and belief. Both will strengthen over time."

"Yeah, sure, whatever you say."

Jack steered the conversation back to the important topic at hand. "You'll need to call him."

"What? Call that Ryan guy? Are you crazy?"

"No, I'm not crazy," he said. "It's your lead."

"The guy was fricken' nuts. He gave off the weirdest vibes. And did you see how he grabbed my arm? That's just too freaky."

"You need to call him," he urged.

"No way!" Vienna spat. "You can't make me call that guy! I didn't sign up to be a part of this."

"You did," Jack's voice said, sounding calm and serene. His voice was no longer coming from the back seat. He was now within her head.

"I don't like your voice in my head." Vienna shoved a finger in her ear and twisted it violently. "Get out!"

"Where else would you like it?" he asked.

"Get out of my head!" Vienna screeched. "You're driving me nuts! And you can't make me call him. I'm not going to be a part of this. Go away!"

"You are a part of this."

"Well, then I quit! Get out of my head and leave me alone!" Vienna waited for an answer. She expected Jack to protest. Instead, there was silence. Well, not complete silence. Vienna waited for a minute or two, and then turned the music back up, blasting it all the way back to her father's house.

Sunday, May 15
Chapter 9

The sunlight streamed in through a gap in the wooden blinds. Vienna watched a scatter of dust floating and sparkling in the light. She felt refreshed as she stretched her arms towards the heavens. Last night was probably the best night's sleep she'd had in a very long time. No bad dreams, no young woman haunting her, and best of all, no Jack to annoy the hell out of her. Ever since she told him to go away, he had.

Maybe he was gone forever, she thought. Maybe I'm no longer a part of this creepiness that had suddenly forced itself upon me.

Later that morning, Vienna poured herself a cup of coffee and sat at the kitchen table with a low fat strawberry yogurt. It was either a yogurt or carrot sticks for breakfast since the cereal was all gone. Vienna opted for a yogurt.

"Hey," Bunny said, entering the kitchen. "I missed you last night."

"Oh," Vienna said, searching with her spoon for the strawberries at the bottom of the plastic cup.

Yesterday after borrowing Bunny's books and spending most of the day researching spirit guides and ghosts, she snuck out of the house that evening without so much as a word to Bunny. She didn't want to have to explain what she was up to. Even though Bunny seemed like the type of person that would understand the need to investigate a dream, she didn't want to get that close to her. The intimate details of her life, such as Jack, for instance, weren't something she felt like sharing with her soon to be stepmother.

"I never even heard you come in," Bunny continued. "You must've had a late night. Does this have anything to do with that guy named Jack that you mentioned?"

"I guess you can say that." Vienna fished another strawberry out of her yogurt. "I ended up at a club called Goldie's on the strip."

"Goldie's," Bunny repeated, pouring coffee into a hot pink mug with a heart-shaped picture of Poopsie, photoshopped onto the front. She shifted Poopsie, who was in his usual place, squished to her bosom, to her other arm. "Hmmm, I don't think I've heard of it."

"I'm not surprised," Vienna said, watching Poopsie squirm, trying to get down.

"Are you hungry, Poopsie-woopsy?" Bunny set the fluffy little dog on the counter near the sink and pulled a lid off a small can of food. She plopped wet stinky beef on a little blue plate for Poopsie to eat then joined Vienna at the table. Vienna wondered how her dad felt about animals eating smelly food off his countertops, but kept her thoughts to herself.

"I have the perfect girl's day planned for us," Bunny said. Her blue eyes gleamed with excitement.

"Oh, uh, really?" Vienna was hoping to have a nice, quiet, somewhat normal day alone, now that Jack was gone. She looked forward to her life going back to both normal and boring.

"Today we're going to have our nails done. I was thinking sometime this afternoon after we have lunch. It's best to have a full stomach when you have your nails done." Bunny held up her hot pink manicured nails and examined them. "I'm in desperate need of a fill. It's been way over two weeks." She glanced at Vienna's short, stubby, unfiled fingernails. "I thought you'd like that, and then…"

Vienna stopped Bunny from continuing, "I keep my nails short on purpose. It's hard to paint with long fingernails. I get paint under them and the pigment seems to stain the acrylic. It's a mess."

"Oh, that's right. You're an artist. That's so neat. Maybe we can get pedicures instead." Bunny slipped a foot out of her sandals and wiggled her petite little toes.

"I try not to draw attention to my Ronald McDonald feet," Vienna joked, lifting a size ten foot, and wiggling her long toes.

"Ronald McDonald feet?" Bunny wrinkled her brow. She didn't seem to get the reference.

"Because they're really big," Vienna explained. "Ronald McDonald is a clown. He wears really big shoes."

"Oh, I see," Bunny giggled. "They're not that big. I think your toenails would look very pretty with a light shade of pink."

"Well, actually," Vienna said, "I'm thinking of getting a flight home today." Vienna stopped herself before stating the reason why. Bunny didn't need to know about the dream and her problems with Jack. But since her problems seemed to be gone now, there really was no reason to stay. She was relieved that Jack actually listened to her and went back to wherever it was he came from. Since there were no more nightmares, there was no more reason for her to investigate. She was off the hook.

"But," Bunny pouted, "what about your dad? He'll be so disappointed if you leave before he sees you. He's looking forward to next weekend."

Vienna had forgotten all about her father flying out to the desert. She wasn't sure if she could stomach seeing her father and Bunny together and all lovey dovey. The thought made her feel sick inside. Nevertheless, she did owe her father a lot, considering he was paying for her schooling, her apartment, and for her unexpected on a whim trip to the desert, as well as many other things. The least she could do was stay for the week, do some pretend girl bonding with Bunny, and then leave on Sunday. She could spend all day Saturday with her father then hop on an airplane first thing Sunday morning. She'd just tell him she had a test Monday morning that she couldn't miss.

Unfortunately, that meant one entire week with Bunny, on top of the days she'd already wasted in the desert. She wasn't sure she could handle that. It wasn't that Bunny was all that bad. She actually rather liked her. It was just weird knowing that soon Bunny would be her stepmother. She didn't want to be friends with her soon to be stepmom. It was just too strange.

"That's true," Vienna said, mulling this over. "I guess my mind has been on my classes," she lied. "I have a test coming up. It's all I can think about."

"That's understandable," Bunny agreed and took a sip

of coffee. "I was an utter mess in college. All I ever did was study, study, and study."

Vienna had a hard time picturing Bunny studying. Bunny and books just didn't seem to go together. "Yeah, I guess I can see that."

"Since you don't want to get your nails done, I'll just get to the big surprise."

"Big surprise?" Vienna scooped the last spoonful of yogurt into her mouth.

"You're going to love it!" Bunny clapped her hands together. "I can't wait!"

"What kind of surprise?"

"You know what? I don't think I'm going to tell you because if I told you, then there'd be no surprise, and I don't want to be the one to spoil it. And who doesn't love a surprise?" she giggled and glanced at her watch. "All I'm going to tell you is that we have an appointment scheduled in about an hour. So go freshen up. We're going to leave in twenty minutes. Okay?"

"Uh, sure."

Bunny hopped up from the table and fled from the room to go get ready for the big surprise forgetting all about poor little Poopsie. Poopsie was still on the countertop. He finished licking every last drop of stinky beef from his plate and was whining, waiting for someone to put him down on the floor.

Vienna lifted the little dog from the counter and set him near his water bowl. She gnawed on her lower lip as she contemplated Bunny's big surprise.

At least it couldn't be as shocking as being haunted by a dead girl in a red dress or being bugged by a hunky spirit guide who annoyed the heck out of her. She headed up to her room to brush her teeth, and run a comb through her unruly mop of hair.

***

Not even twenty minutes later, Vienna found herself driving up into the mountains of the hi-desert in Bunny's silver Mercedes. Bunny was the driver, and Vienna, the prisoner. About half an hour later, they were sitting in the lobby of a small building with a huge, colorful mural of a palm painted onto the outside of the stucco structure.

Bunny had scheduled them to have private readings with her all time favorite psychic, Clara. That was her big surprise. And Vienna had to admit, she was surprised. This was the last thing she'd ever expected. She would've expected hair appointments, or makeovers, not psychic readings. The thought made her feel nervous.

Vienna walked around the little shop and studied the shelves. One shelf that drew her attention had beautiful figurines of angels of all kinds. The shelf beneath it had different colored crystals and rocks. Little note cards were placed by each type of gem explaining what the rock was and what kind of energy it held.

Next to the rocks was a basket with a variety of incense. Vienna sniffed the vanilla scented one. She'd always liked the scent of vanilla. For some reason, vanilla made her feel calm. She remembered how she used to wear vanilla scented perfume when she was in junior high. It was her absolute favorite.

Music jingled from Vienna's purse bringing her back from her memories of middle school. She dug her phone out. It was both playing music and vibrating to let her know she had an incoming call. Cautiously, she glanced at the screen. The last thing she needed was a spiritual phone call from Jack.

"It's my friend, Kim," she told Bunny who was glancing over Vienna's shoulder at the phone.

"Hello." Vienna took a seat on a brown sofa against a wall. A small round table with an oversized white doily draped over it and a miniature rock waterfall was at one end. A wooden rocking chair was at the other end.

"Hey, are you coming back soon or do I have to teach class again today?"

"Yeah, I'm sorry, Kim. I'll be back soon. Promise." Vienna studied a framed poster of an angel with blue wings and beautiful pink gown on the wall across from her. "It looks like I'll be back home sometime on Sunday. My Dad flies in on Friday night. That way I'll have at least one full day to spend with him before flying home."

"So, what was that guy's name again? You know, the one that kind of stood you up. The really good looking one."

Vienna was silent. She knew whom Kim was referring to and she really didn't want to discuss Jack.

"Have you heard from him again?" Kim asked. She loved gossip especially if it involved good-looking guys. "Come on, you've gotta give me something."

"Yeah, I have," Vienna said, not wanting to discuss it further. The less she thought of Jack, the better.

"Well…" Kim coaxed. "Come on, details…"

"Oh, it's our turn," Bunny said, when a middle-aged woman with long silver braids, who Vienna guessed was Clara, appeared from behind a closed door. A heavyset woman with short brown hair whom was dabbing at her eyes with a tissue, followed. They walked past the lobby where Bunny and Vienna were sitting and the heavyset

103

woman hugged Clara then left.

"Um, I've gotta go," Vienna told Kim.

"What? Without giving me some juicy details? That's so not fair."

"Bunny scheduled us some appointments. It's our turn. I'll call you back. Promise."

Kim wasn't going to let Vienna off that easily. She could tell when Vienna was being evasive. "What kind of appointments?"

Vienna turned her back and lowered her voice to not be overheard as Bunny talked to Clara. "Psychic readings."

"What?" Kim squealed. "That is so cool!"

"You don't think it's weird?" Vienna whispered.

"No, I think it's awesome! I love the supernatural!"

"Really?" Vienna's voice rose. "Since when?"

"Since always!" she said. "It's something I didn't think you'd understand. So I just don't talk about it with you. This is so cool. I had no idea you believed in psychic stuff."

"I don't," Vienna said. "Well, I don't know. I'm still skeptical."

"Call me and let me know how it goes."

"You're kidding, right?" Vienna asked. She suddenly felt like she didn't even know her best friend. How could she not know that Kim believed in the supernatural?

"Do I ever kid?" she laughed. "I'll forgive you for making me teach alone."

Vienna laughed. "Okay. Deal."

Bunny waved a hand at Vienna to follow her into the other room.

"Okay, gotta go now."

"Call me."

"I will." Vienna pushed the little red phone icon, hanging up. She then shut her phone off just in case Jack got the sudden urge to send her a text message during her reading. She wasn't going to let him push himself into her life. As far as she was concerned, she had had enough of the supernatural.

Vienna was ushered by Bunny to a round table with a forest green tablecloth and cream-colored upholstered rolling chairs. The walls had been painted a neutral tan color with crisp white trim. Several framed posters of mystical looking waterfalls in beautiful surroundings were hanging on the walls. A potted palm tree was set in one corner of the room.

For being a small stucco building with a tacky painting of a palm on the side of it in the middle of nowhere, the inside was actually quite comfortable and roomy. Another rock waterfall was placed near the door, tinkling lightly, emitting a calm relaxing vibe.

Vienna felt that this room would be the perfect environment for creative thought to manifest. She could picture herself spending many hours in here, drawing and painting.

Clara smiled at Vienna and took a seat in a plush chair across the table from both she and Bunny. She had a deck of oversized navy blue cards with gold trim that she was shuffling. After a few shuffles, she slid the deck over to Vienna.

Vienna stared at her blankly.

"This is her first tarot card reading," Bunny said.

"Just shuffle the cards any way you'd like, dear," Clara instructed. "The cards pick up your energy."

105

"Okay," Vienna said, picking up the deck and just kind of cutting it in half and fanning the cards back together, then molding them into a full deck again. She did it a few times, shrugged, and then pushed the deck back over to Clara.

"Go ahead and cut the deck," she instructed.

"Okay." Feeling the cards with her fingers, Vienna lifted about twenty cards and then set them down in their own pile.

"Perfect." Clara took the cards, restacking them where the cards were cut with the bottom half on top. From the pile, she started taking one card at a time, flipping them over, and setting them down in a pattern.

"Hmmm… hmmm…" she hummed thoughtfully, several times while studying each card before carefully placing them on the table.

Waiting for what the psychic had to say about the cards was really making Vienna feel anxious. Her palms were beginning to sweat and she rubbed them on her jeans.

Not that she'd ever admit to even thinking that a person could be psychic or could read the future from a stack of cards. It just didn't seem possible.

"I see a man," Clara said.

Bunny beamed at Vienna, lifting her thin tweezed eyebrows.

A man, that's pretty vague, Vienna thought, not at all impressed.

"I get the letter J." Clara had her eyes closed as if picturing this man in her mind.

Lots of men have names that start with the letter J, thought Vienna. *Big deal.*

"He's handsome in a boyish sort of way," Clara continued. "You know what I mean? Nice eyes. Sandy hair. He's smirking right now."

I bet he is, Vienna scowled. She turned to look at Bunny who mouthed the name, Jack.

Vienna shook her head, not wanting to let Jack back in her life. She refused to let him in. He needed to go away and leave her alone.

Bunny nodded. As far as Bunny knew, Jack was some good looking human guy that Vienna had been talking to.

Vienna shook her head no and flashed Bunny the evil eye.

"He has a message for you," Clara continued, unaware of Vienna and Bunny's silent argument. "He said to pay attention. Does that mean anything to you?"

Clara opened her eyes and made eye contact with Vienna. "You have a mission," she said. She looked down at the cards scrawled on the table before her. Her index finger landed on the Death card. "This card right here means the death of the old. What I'm getting is that your life is changing. You are at a crossroads. The old life will be left behind for the new life ahead. Does this make any sense to you?"

"No," Vienna said, stubbornly. "I'm an art student and I teach painting lessons to children. I don't see anything changing at least for another year or so. When I graduate, I plan on working in a studio full time. Not much of a change."

"The cards say otherwise. You have a calling. And it's time."

"What if I don't want this so called change?" Vienna

demanded.

"Life has a way of putting you on track."

Vienna shook her head. "I'm not buying it."

"Vienna," Bunny said, her voice full of concern. "What's wrong?"

It took Vienna a second to realize that she was crying. Tears were clouding her eyes and tumbling down her face.

"You charted this life," Clara said. "This card, the Knight of Swords, is the man I see. The one with the J. This card over here, this represents you. See this card in the middle?"

Vienna wiped at her eyes with the back of her hand. She studied the card and nodded.

"This is your pact. Your destiny."

"What about free will? Don't we all have free will to choose what we want and who we are? Don't I get to shape my own life by my choices?"

"Yes," Clara agreed. "We all have free will."

"Then I'm going to be in charge of my life. I never signed up for some stupid pact. I'm an artist and a teacher. That's my life. And that's what I want."

Clara smiled. "This is the road you've chosen. You had the free will to make this pact."

"But I haven't. I never…" More tears flooded Vienna's eyes. She took off her tear stained glasses and rubbed at her eyes. "I want to leave," she said, getting up from the table.

"Vienna," Bunny cried.

Vienna wrenched the door open, not looking back. She could hear Bunny apologizing to Clara, exchanging a few words that Vienna couldn't hear over her uncontrollable sniffling, before entering the lobby.

Bunny put her arm around Vienna's shoulders. "I'm so sorry, Vienna. I thought you'd enjoy this." She walked Vienna to the car and opened the passenger door for her. "I really wanted us to have a good time."

"I'm sorry," Vienna muttered, when Bunny started up the car. "I don't know what came over me. I just got so... well... emotional."

"No need to explain. I shouldn't have made this appointment. I just thought that maybe you and I found something we could bond over. You know, girl time."

They drove down through the winding hi-desert mountains, from Morongo Valley towards Palm Springs, in complete silence. Bunny hadn't even turned on the stereo. Her mind seemed preoccupied and her eyes stayed focused on the road. When they finally reached the wind belt that adorned hundreds of windmills on the low rolling hills of the low desert near Desert Hot Springs, Vienna finally broke the silence.

"Bunny," she cleared her throat, "what she had said was true."

"Clara?" Bunny asked, glancing at Vienna over the top of her oversized black sunglasses.

Vienna nodded. "I think she just hit a little too close to home. It's just, well, she said some things that I don't want to hear. I just want you to know, it's not your fault. I mean, you making this appointment. It's really not your fault. You were just trying to do something nice for me."

Bunny seemed relieved. "I believe everything happens for a reason, Vienna. Maybe this was something you needed to hear. God works in mysterious ways."

"Yeah, I guess so."

They drove the rest of the way home in silence, but it

was no longer an uncomfortable silence.

***

Vienna unfolded the yellow flyer with Ryan's phone number on it. She wondered if she should she call him.

If this truly was her calling, if she was for some reason supposed to help this girl that was murdered, she had nothing else to go on, but this phone number.

She held up her cell phone and typed in the phone number on the screen, but before pushing send, she suddenly had the urge to call Kim. Kim was a lot more open minded than she'd ever believed. She had been completely floored at Kim's openness about her having a psychic reading.

"I'll call her," she said, aloud. After all, Kim was her best friend and best friends were supposed to be able to talk to each other about anything and everything.

Feeling relieved at putting off the phone call to Ryan, Vienna scrolled down her contact list until she reached Kim's photo and pushed send.

"Hey, Vienna," Kim said, answering on the first ring. "Tell me all about it. No leaving anything out."

"Aren't you busy with homework or something?"

"Or something," Kim laughed. "I'm watching TV and eating a roll of chocolate chip cookie dough for dinner."

"And you didn't invite me?"

"Hey now, you didn't invite me to Palm Springs. I could be doing some serious shopping right about now."

Kim had an addiction to shopping. Every single penny was spent before she'd even earned it. It was an addiction that Kim had inherited from her mother. The two of them were shopping divas. Like mother, like daughter. One of these days, she expected to see them on an episode of Clean House. The crew would come in and climb over the mounds and mounds of shopping mess and then clean out their clutter and redecorate, starting by scratch.

Vienna decided to tell Kim everything. She left no stone unturned. Not only did she tell her all about her tarot card reading, she told her all about Jack, the reoccurring dream, the dead woman in the red dress, the dumpster, her adventure at Goldie's Club, and creepy Ryan.

Kim was the quietest she'd probably ever been in her entire life. She didn't even interrupt to ask questions or to give input on what Vienna was telling her. All she did was listen, which was quite out of the ordinary.

"You still there?" Vienna asked when she finished. She was worried that Kim wouldn't believe her, or that she would think she needed psychiatric help or something.

"I'm coming out there," Kim said.

"What?" This was not what she'd expected to hear. In fact, she expected Kim to bombard her with questions and comments like; what in the world is happening to you? Are you crazy? You've just been having bad dreams, not premonitions. Dead people are not communicating with you. All this must be due to the stress of college life.

"I'm coming out there," she said, again. "You're not going to go out with that Ryan guy on your own. You need back up."

"Back up?" Vienna was thrown for a loop.

"Yup. And who else better to trust than your best friend. I'll make a fantastic sidekick."

"Sidekick? What are you talking about? This isn't

111

some kind of superhero movie."

Kim groaned. "Vienna, you have a ghost trying to communicate with you, a spirit guide trying to guide you, but no real flesh in blood to help you. This is an investigation, a paranormal investigation, and I want to help."

"A paranormal, what? I've never heard of anything like that before. Besides, don't you have a Spanish test coming up?"

"Nah," Kim said. Vienna could picture her waving her hand nonchalantly. "I've flunked the last two tests, anyhow. Missing this one isn't going to matter. I probably need to retake the course, anyway."

"But it's senior year," Vienna said. She'd be paranoid if she were flunking a class. "What are you going to do? Don't you need that class to graduate? Can't you take the test online?"

"Yeah, I can take it online. But I doubt I'll pass." Kim laughed. She never panicked when it came to school and grades. "If I don't, I'll just make it up in summer school. No biggie. Besides, you need my gear."

"Gear?" Vienna asked. "What gear?"

"Don't you know anything about the paranormal? Do you even watch TV?"

"You know I watch TV." Vienna was feeling personally attacked. "Just not that kind of stuff."

"Girl, you've been so sheltered."

"I have not!"

"In this aspect you have. It's time to start seeing the world in vivid color and no longer with those black and white blinders on. You're an artist at heart and an artist needs to be open."

"I'm open," Vienna said, defensively. "Jeez." She'd never thought of herself as seeing things in black and white. She'd always thought she was an open person. Knowing that all this time Kim, her best friend in the whole world, thought of her as closed minded, stung a bit.

"Yeah, okay," Kim said, full of sarcasm. "You're open."

"Well," Vienna thought about it for a second, "open to a point."

"Well, regardless of whether or not you're open and receiving, you need paranormal gear. It'll help in the investigation."

"And you have this paranormal gear stuff?"

"Of course," Kim said. "I bought the coolest gadgets online. They had this huge sale at this one website I found called Ghost Hunters."

"Have you used this gear before?" Vienna knew that no matter what, Kim could never pass up a good sale. Many items she purchased were never opened. They just ended up in the storage room or stashed in a closet somewhere in her Mom's house. Once or twice a year they had a huge yard sale to unload things to make room for new things. Between the two of them, Vienna felt they could easily open up their own mall.

"No, not yet. It's stashed around here somewhere. But no worries, I'll find it. I think I remember where I put the boxes. Like I said, I bought the coolest stuff. It's all the latest in techno gadgets and guaranteed to work."

"What about our art class? Who's going to teach it if we're both gone?"

"Heather can."

"Heather can't," Vienna disputed. Heather was

Kim's older sister and a history major. "She doesn't know anything about art. And besides, what makes you think she'd want to teach it?"

"She's looking for a part time job. I'll give her fifty bucks for the week. It's only for three classes. And the kids are on autopilot, anyway. All she has to do is make sure they don't eat the paint or shove paintbrushes up their noses for a couple of hours. No big deal."

Vienna sighed. Kim was right. Their job was no big deal. A monkey could teach the class. The kids already knew the basics and spent the entire two-hour class just doing their own creative paintings. From time to time, they'd get a beginner in the class, but as of right now, all of the children enrolled were advanced painters. "So, when are you coming out?"

"Hmmm, good question."

Vienna could practically hear the gears in Kim's brain turning as she planned this out. She could just picture her looking at her watch and counting the hours on her fingers.

"How about I catch the first flight out tomorrow morning? That'll give me just enough time to pack and find my gear. All I need to do is go online and book a flight. I'll text you on when to pick me up at the airport."

"Sounds good. Just try and make it not too early, okay? I'd rather it was a late morning flight." Vienna wasn't known for being a morning person like Kim was. Kim bounced out of bed every morning around five no matter what time she'd gone to bed the night before. She never needed caffeine, and was always perky. Vienna was quite the opposite.

"Okay, I'll probably need some beauty rest after all

my packing tonight, anyhow. Oh, and, I hate to ask you this, but could I borrow some money for the tickets. All my credit cards are kind of maxed out. I can pay you back after payday. Promise."

Vienna grinned. Kim was notorious for having no cash on hand except after her and her mother's big yearly yard sale. And that never lasted long.

"Sure. No problem. I'll go online and book your flight," Vienna offered. She figured that having Kim come out would be very convenient so she wouldn't be alone in the house with Bunny. She knew that Kim would make a decent buffer so this next week shouldn't be too bad after all.

"Thanks so much. I promise to pay you back ASAP."

"No worries. I'll have the tickets emailed to you. Okay?"

"Awesome! Thanks. See you en la Mañana."

"Okay, bye."

Monday, May 16
Chapter 10

Last night had been quite uneventful and for the most part, quiet. Vienna and Bunny had sat in silence and watched television. Vienna munched on a bag of tortilla chips and Bunny snacked on carrot sticks. Not once did Bunny bring up Vienna's tarot card reading. Vienna was surprised that she didn't even try to pry. And when Vienna told her about her friend, Kim, coming out for a visit, Bunny didn't question that either. In fact, she seemed excited that more company was coming to stay and couldn't wait to entertain.

At around ten thirty, they decided to call it a night. Vienna crawled into bed and read a few pages of a good mystery novel she'd been reading on her kindle app on her phone until she drifted off to sleep. Nothing out of the ordinary happened. No bad dreams and no sign of Jack.

In the morning, Vienna woke up feeling refreshed and energized. She couldn't help but wonder if Kim's flight to the desert would be a wasted venture. But no matter what, she was happy that her friend was coming out. They'd have a good time whether it involved the paranormal or not.

Sitting in the little café next to the glass doors that the passengers had to go through in order to enter the airport; Vienna sipped a small mocha with extra whip cream, and watched the passengers file in. When she had first arrived at the airport, she double-checked Kim's flight schedule on one of the television monitors. It was going to be right on time.

She glanced at her watch. Kim would be disembarking at any moment.

Vienna got up and walked to the entrance area where a small group of people were forming to meet their loved ones as they arrived.

Over the years, she'd done a lot of traveling to and from Palm Springs and knew that it took a little while to walk from where the planes were landing to the front of the airport.

The indoor portion of the airport itself wasn't very large. But from where the planes landed to the building itself was a nice little outdoor venture. Since the weather was generally mild in the winter being that Palm Springs is in the middle of the southern California desert, there weren't many problems with having part of your walk outdoors.

During the summer, misters would be running to keep people from overheating and during the winter heat lamps kept people from getting too chilly. This was how the desert was set up. Even at all of the outdoor restaurants, bars, and shopping areas.

Vienna spotted Kim sporting a large pink and black, flower printed carryon. She was wearing her blonde streaked locks pulled up in a loose bun, secured with giant black bobby pins. And resting on her petite nose was a pair of oversized designer sunglasses. If Vienna hadn't known better, she would've mistaken her glamorous best friend for a movie star. Kim was wearing powder pink Capri's, a white formfitting tank top and white three-inch high-heeled strappy sandals. The light colors showed off her tanning bed, bronzed skin.

Kim wiggled her digits at Vienna. Her short pink fingernails matched her outfit. "Vienna!" she screeched as if they hadn't seen each other in years.

"Kim!" she screeched back and gave her friend a hug and air kisses on each cheek. "You look as fabulous as ever!"

They both laughed at the inside joke. The screeching was something they did on campus whenever they went an hour or so without seeing each other. It started out as being a way to make fun of the popular girls involved in snooty sororities. Personally, Vienna had no problem with girls joining sororities. She really didn't. But she did have a problem with the sorority girls that judged people on outside appearances, or the ones that would only let you in if your parents made a certain amount of money. That was just wrong.

She and Kim had decided to join a sorority their freshmen year. Vienna was accepted, but Kim wasn't. She had to do a little snooping to find out why. And when she found out that Kim was rejected due to the annual income of her parents, Vienna turned the sorority down.

Vienna watched as Kim rounded up her luggage. Kim grabbed hold of a decent sized suitcase and yanked.

"That one, too," she said, pointing to another pink

and black flower print suitcase that was closer to Vienna.

"Dang, girl," Vienna huffed as she took hold of it by the handle and dragged the jumbo-sized case off the conveyer belt. "This weighs a ton. How much stuff did you bring?"

"That's all." Kim smiled. "I couldn't decide what all I should bring. You know, in case I need to dress up and all. Oh, and some of the stuff I packed for you, too."

"Oh, yeah, the gear," Vienna said. She towed the hefty suitcase on its wheels and walked in the direction of the large glass double doors. "I parked out that way."

Kim followed, pulling the matching medium sized case and carrying both her purse and her carryon on her left shoulder. "I brought you clothes, too."

"Clothes? For me?"

"Well, yeah," Kim said.

Vienna smiled. She didn't even bother to ask her to elaborate.

***

Vienna thought it would only be fair to invite Bunny out to lunch with them. Surprisingly, the three of them had a really good time. Kim and Bunny seemed to have a lot to talk about and Vienna enjoyed listening. She was thankful that neither Bunny nor Kim brought up psychics, tarot cards, ghosts, or anything paranormal. They kept the conversation wrapped around clothing, fashion, and shopping.

Vienna really didn't have much to say about any of the above. It wasn't that she didn't like clothing, fashion, and shopping, she did. It's just that those topics didn't really interest her in the ways that they interested both Bunny and Kim. Not enough to have a long conversation about it. She was one of those shoppers that shopped because she needed or wanted something like for example; a new pair of jeans. She'd enter the department store and try on the items, only if she had to, then bought them and left. That's it. It was a very simple and painless process, as simple as one, two, and three. No real thought or effort involved.

After lunch, and a girl's day of perusing the Cabazon Outlets because Kim promised to check on a certain pair of jeans for sale at the Levi's outlet for her mother, they went back to Vienna's dad's house. Kim followed Vienna up the stairs to the guest room next door to Vienna's room. It was the room her brother stayed in when he visited.

"Ooooh," Kim said, as they entered the room. She walked around, admiring the blue paint and oak furniture. "So this is the inside of Jared's room."

Vienna rolled her eyes. Kim has had a major crush on her brother for quite some time now. Twice Kim had come out to stay in the desert with Vienna, but this was the first time she'd occupied this particular room.

"Not technically," Vienna reminded. "It's just a guest room, remember? This is a vacation house."

"I remember," Kim sighed, plopping down on the bed. "A girl can dream, can't she?"

"He's not all that," Vienna said, still struggling with the enormous flowered suitcase. She had lugged it up the stairs and was a bit out of breath by the time they reached Kim's room. "Where do you want it?"

Kim pointed to the other two suitcases that she set down near the door when they entered. "Over there is fine. So, what are we doing tonight?"

Vienna shrugged. "Ouch," she grabbed her left shoulder and reached for the knot behind the blade. "Your suitcase just about killed me."

"Why don't you call that guy, you know, what's his name?"

"Ryan?"

"Yeah, Ryan," Kim repeated. "Set a date up with him."

"And then what?"

"You pump him for information and I follow you to make sure he's a good boy."

"I don't know. I don't feel comfortable with that. He's kind of creepy."

"Hmmm, I guess you could tell him you have a friend in town and see if he's got any cute guy friends. We can double date."

"Kim, Ryan's friend killed a girl. Or at least I think so." Vienna plopped down on the bed next to Kim and sighed. "In my dreams, anyway."

"Hmmm…" Kim sulked. "I guess that's kinda creepy. But look on the bright side, he didn't do it. His friend did it. So he should be harmless."

"Should be," Vienna said. "But what if he's not? What if he's just like his friend? What if he was in on it?"

"What if, what if, what if? You can *what if* forever and never get any answers. And didn't you say they worked together? They were coworkers?"

"Yeah."

"Okay, then, that doesn't mean they were close friends. They could've been nothing more than two guys that worked together."

"True." Vienna nodded. The thought of them just

being coworkers really seemed to calm her nerves. Just because Ryan would go out for drinks after work with a coworker doesn't mean that he was a friend.

"So give him a call," Kim urged.

Vienna sucked in a deep breath and got up from the bed. "Okay," she said exhaling, "let me get my phone. I have his number in my room."

"Awesome!" Kim gave her a thumbs up and flashed a brilliant smile.

Vienna was relieved when she got Ryan's voicemail because she really didn't want to talk to him. Her first instinct when she heard his prerecorded voice had been to hang up, but instead she forced herself to wait for the beep and leave a message. Leaving messages was something she hated doing. For some strange reason she had a tendency to stutter or stumbled over her words. She did the same thing when having to give speeches or speak in front of a group of people.

She kept her message short and to the point. "Hi, Ryan. This is Vienna. We met at Goldie's the other night. Just wanted to give you a call. Bye."

Vienna knocked on Kim's door.

"Come in."

"Hey, I left a message," she said, upon entering, phone in hand.

Kim was going through her luggage and unpacking her clothes. "I have a few things that will wrinkle if I don't hang them up right away."

Vienna nodded, thinking of her duffle bag sitting on the floor in the corner of her bedroom. All her clothes were either in the bag or thrown on the floor in a jumbled mess. Hanging them up hadn't even occurred to her.

"Okay," Kim said while hanging her clothes in the empty closet. "I was just thinking of an alternative plan in case you don't hear back from Ryan. Is it okay if I put some things in the dresser, too?"

Vienna slid open one of the oak drawers. It was empty. "Sure, I don't see why not."

"Thanks." Kim carried over socks, underwear, and lingerie and put them in the drawer. "I was thinking," she continued, "that we could go to the club where you saw the girl in your dreams."

"Goldie's?"

"Yeah." She made a second trip from her open suitcase to the dresser and filled another drawer. "Maybe we'll run into Ryan there or get some vibes or something."

"Maybe."

"Speaking of vibes, have you spoken to your hunky spirit guide?"

"Jack's not hunky," Vienna huffed.

"I'll take that as a no. Well, maybe you should try apologizing to him. That might make him reappear."

"Apologize to him?" Vienna snapped. That really struck a nerve. "Why should I apologize to him?"

"For telling him to go away." Kim pulled out her hot pink makeup bag. "I'm going to put this in the bathroom." She looked around. "This room doesn't have its own bathroom, does it?"

"You can use the one in the hall or if you want, you can share with me."

Kim set the bag down on top of the dresser. "I'll just leave it in here for now."

"I did nothing wrong," Vienna continued. "Jack had no right to invade my space, especially talking in my head.

It's one thing for him to talk to me; it's another for him to talk in my head. It's rude. A girl needs her privacy."

"Well, apologize anyway. He probably didn't know."

"No." Vienna crossed her arms over her chest. "I won't apologize. He had no right to do that to me."

Kim was now unloading shoes and lining them up on the top shelf in the closet. "You just need to set up ground rules. If he's going to help with the investigation then he needs to follow your guidelines. That's all."

As corny as the whole investigation thing sounded to Vienna, she liked Kim's idea of guidelines. It might just work. "I don't know. I'll think about it."

Kim smiled. She zipped up the now empty suitcase and replaced it with the larger of the two cases. "Just get a load of this," she said, green eyes sparkling. Unzipping the suitcase she squealed, "You're going to love it!"

Vienna crawled up onto the bed and leaned back against the pillows as her friend pulled out a sleek formfitting black leather jacket.

"Do you like it?" she asked, slipping it on.

Vienna had to admit that the jacket was stunning. "Wow. It's gorgeous!"

"I know! Isn't it?" Kim reached into her luggage and pulled out a matching jacket in a larger size. "I'm glad you like it because I have one for you, too."

Kim was only about 5'2 and small boned and wore a size 3 on a bad day, where Vienna was 5'6 and average in build. She generally wore a size 7, sometimes a 10. It depended on the brand and style of the clothing. Vienna examined the jacket. The tags were still attached.

"When did you get these?" she asked.

"A while ago. That one was for my mom. We

bought matching outfits, but they've never been worn.
She said I can give it to you because she'll probably never
get around to wearing it. She has another 20 lbs or so to
lose first."

Vienna slipped the jacket on. It fit perfectly.

"And I have these," she said, pulling out black leather
pants to match the jackets. "And I brought black stretchy
tops for both of us. We'll look so hot investigating in
these."

Vienna ran her fingers over the leather. It was the
softest leather she'd ever felt in her life. "This isn't a
fashion show," she joked. "I don't think it matters what
we wear."

"Oh, I know," Kim said with a wave of a hand. "But
a girl should always dress for success just in case. You
never know what can happen or who you might run into."

Vienna laughed.

***

Vienna hadn't received a call back from Ryan. Inside
she was secretly happy. She kept her feelings to herself
because she didn't want Kim to know what a chicken she
was. A surge of relief washed over her at the thought of
no communication with Ryan. She had absolutely no
desire to speak with him, ever. It actually gnawed away at
her insides that Ryan would now have her cell phone
number because she had called and left him a message.
There was just something about the guy that gave her the
heebie jeebies.

My dream, she thought. This is so silly. Kim and I
are dressed in black leather, cruising down Palm Canyon
drive in the middle of the night in search of a man that
may have killed a woman because I dreamt it. I really am

nuts. Oh, great, so is Kim.

Vienna slowly inched her car down Palm Canyon in search of the tourist shop with the T-shirts in the display window that she'd parked in front of when she was there Saturday night. Being that it was now a weeknight, the street was dotted with only a few tourists here and there, so she could take all the time she needed looking for a place to park. No stream of cars was backed up behind her making her feel anxious about driving too slow. Spotting the shop, Vienna pulled into the same parking space next to the bench in front of the store. "Okay," she said. "This is it. This where I parked last time."

"Cool," Kim said, unlatching her seatbelt. "Oh, look at that shirt. The green one with the rhinestones is so cute!"

Vienna wrinkled her nose and gave Kim a look.

"I know, I know," Kim said. "We're not here to shop."

"It's not only that," Vienna said. "Would you really want to wear a Palm Springs tourist shirt?"

Kim shrugged. "Sure, if it's cute. Why not?"

The girls strolled down the street in the direction of Goldie's, retracing Vienna's footsteps from last time. She was now kicking herself for parking so far away. Why didn't she search for a parking spot near the club? The street was vacant. Finding a place to park near Goldie's would've been no big deal.

When they finally reached the large wooden door of the club, Vienna tried the handle. It was locked. She knocked on the front door. Nothing. She put her ear to the wood and listened. Still nothing. Not even music. The place was dark, quiet and felt deserted.

"I guess they're closed on Mondays," Vienna said with a shrug. "Now what?"

"What about the dumpster in the alley? The one you think the girl was murdered at? Didn't you say it's nearby?"

Vienna shook her head. "No, no, no… I don't want to go there."

"Come on," Kim said. "How do you expect us to communicate with her if we don't try?"

"Communicate with us?"

"Yeah, sure." Kim was digging in her black leather bag that was slung over her shoulder. "You wouldn't expect me to be ghost hunting without my special gadgets, would you?"

"Ghost hunting?" Vienna had to laugh. "Who said anything about ghost hunting?"

"You won't be laughing when we find her and communicate with her."

"I don't know." Vienna was still shaking her head. The entire ghost-slash-murder-thing still seemed so absurd.

"What's the worst that can happen?" Kim asked, holding up a navy blue rectangular gadget with a rounded red top. "We get scared?"

"I can black out and hit my head. It happened last time." The gadget Kim was holding had a white monitor and black numbers printed on the face in the shape of an arc. A little red needle was pointing to zero. Vienna leaned in to get a better look. "What's that?"

"An EMF detector," Kim said proudly, handing the object to Vienna.

Vienna ran her finger over the words, The Ghost

Meter, printed in white on the front of the device. "An EMF detector?"

"An electromagnetic field detector."

"And what does it do?" Vienna placed her finger over the zero that the little red needle was pointing to.

"It detects energy fields that ghosts put off. As long as no other things are putting out EMFs around us, then we know it's a ghost. It'll detect other energy sources, too. So you kind of have to watch for fluctuations."

"And that will help us, how?"

"If the needle spikes and there are no active outlets or electricity nearby then we know we're not really imagining what we're feeling or seeing," Kim said, smugly. "We'll have proof that we're not nuts. You know, we'll know there's actually something in front of us. We'll have scientific evidence."

"How do you know about this stuff?"

"I watch TV," Kim answered. "Come on, let's go find a ghost."

"I don't know." Vienna gnawed on her lower lip. She knew they were only a block or two away from the alley with the dumpster where she believed the girl was murdered. She mulled this over for a bit. Kim was staring at her waiting for an answer. She didn't want to upset her friend who flew all the way out here just to help her. Kim actually believed her, when she knew how ridiculous she sounded. Not once did she question Vienna's story about the ghost in the red dress, or Jack, her dreams, or her psychic reading. The least she could do was humor Kim even if nothing came of it. Kim was obviously being a good friend and trying to help her. So what if they found nothing? But then again, what if they did find something?

Maybe the latter of the two was what was causing her to hesitate.

Vienna did a mental shrug. They might as well check it out. After all, they were prepared for investigating the paranormal. As prepared as two amateur ghost chasing girls could be. They were sporting new black leather outfits and toting ghost hunting gear around, so they might as well put their gadgets to good use. What was the worst that could happen?

"Okay," Vienna said with more determination than she felt. "Let's go find us a ghost."

***

"It's down there." Vienna pointed down the street towards the dark alley. They were a few feet away and she could already feel the negative energy surrounding them. It was a heavy foreboding feeling that weighed on her shoulders and felt heavy in her chest. She wondered if Kim could feel it, but didn't want to ask. She peeked around the corner. A small stream of light from the moon lit up a corner of the dumpster.

"Creepy," Kim said, holding out her EMF detector. "Kinda dark."

"Yup," Vienna agreed, glancing over Kim's shoulder trying to get a look at the detector. She could barely see the screen.

"Still at zero," Kim said. "Are you feeling anything?"

Vienna was feeling apprehensive because she was frightened. But she didn't want Kim to know how scared she was. She wondered if this was the time to bring up the negative energy. Probably not. Better to keep that inside, in case she was just imagining it. "Nope, nothing."

"Let's get closer."

129

"Um, yeah, sure."

Kim was already walking towards the dumpster. Vienna sucked in air and followed. Kim stopped at the corner of the dumpster where the moon was lighting it up. She squinted at the EMF detector. "Still nada."

Vienna peered over her shoulder to take a look. Nothing was moving. The little needle still pointed to the zero. Kim reached into her purse and pulled out a small flashlight attached to her key chain. She shined the light on the screen of the EMF detector as she explored every inch of the dark alley. After what felt like ages to Vienna, Kim said, "I'm not getting anything. I wonder if it's broken."

"Did you test it to make sure it works?"

"I tried it at your house and it worked fine. I held it up to the lamp and then in the kitchen I tried the refrigerator and the needle moved. But who knows? I guess I should've bought one of those new digital ones."

"They have digital ones?"

"Yeah, but they weren't on sale. I got a package deal on the clearance page. And I didn't really think I'd use it, anyways. I just thought it would be neat to have. You know, just in case."

Kim joined Vienna who was still standing near the corner of the dumpster. For some reason the moonlight made her feel safe. The dark corners of the alley terrified her. It was irrational to feel afraid of the dark, but she couldn't help the way she felt. The light comforted her in a weird sort of way.

"Should we go now?" she asked, hoping that Kim would've already satisfied her ghost hunting needs.

"No. I think we should give it more time."

"And do what? Just stand here?"

"Hmmm." Kim shined her tiny flashlight on the ground and looked around the alley some more while she thought. "Maybe I can find a box or something we can sit on. Oh, wait a minute! Vienna!"

"What?" Vienna jumped at Kim's excitement. "What is it?"

"A spike. I got a spike! It jumped to two. Now it's at a four. Oh, my God, Vienna, get over here!" Kim waved her hand. "Hurry! It's so cold! I've got goose bumps. Do you feel it? It's amazing!"

Vienna sprinted to Kim's side. The familiar gust of cold air tussled her hair, slightly blowing it away from her face. Cold encompassed her entire body giving her chills that ripped through her stomach and traveled from head to toe. "Yeah, I feel it. It's her."

"I know. I can feel her energy," Kim said. "It's so intense. She's sad. Here hold this." She shoved the EMF detector, which was spiking to high levels, into Vienna's trembling hands and began to rummage through her purse. The red needle was flittering back and forth.

"Stay with us," Kim said to the coldness around them. "Don't go away. We want to talk with you." She extracted a small slim rectangular object and held it out in front of her. A little red light blinked.

"What is that?" Vienna whispered. She was afraid if she spoke too loud, her voice would frighten the ghost away.

"An EVP recorder."

"A what?"

"It's an electronic voice phenomenon recorder. You know, basically a digital recorder. Just more sensitive than

131

a regular tape recorder. According to what I read on the box, it should be able to pick up a ghost's voice if it can gather enough energy waves to make sound." Kim pushed a button and asked, "What's your name? Speak into this device I'm holding. It can record your voice. That way we can communicate with you."

A vision of the young woman from Vienna's dreams flashed before her eyes. She was wearing the red dress. The same dress from her nightmare. Her dark hair was flowing down her back. Her eyes were big and soulful. Her full lips were soft looking and pouting. She was sad, extremely sad. Tears pricked at Vienna's eyes. She could feel the girl's pain, her anger, her frustration. For some reason the name, Sarah, came to mind but she wasn't sure why. Maybe it was her name. Vienna blinked hard to push away the vision. She felt her imagination was getting the better of her.

"Were you murdered?" Kim asked. "Please talk into this device. Don't be afraid." She moved the recorder in the air, holding it further away. "Did a man kill you? What's his name?"

"Were you wearing a red dress?" Vienna asked, wanting confirmation about her visions. "Did you go to Goldie's?" She paused for a moment between each question and listened, but heard nothing. "Are you the girl in my dream?"

"Do you know that you're dead?" Kim still held the recorder out in front of her hoping to catch an answer. Nothing seemed to be happening.

"Why are you here?" Vienna strained to hear something, anything. But there was still nothing. Only silence and an icy chill were in the air, swirling all around her. She glanced at the EMF detector. The little needle was still spiking, but not as rapidly or as high. The needle pretty much stayed at a two and jumped from time to time to a four then went right back to a two.

Kim slowly turned and pointed the recorder in the direction of the dumpster hoping that she could get something. "Give us a sign that you're here with us. Anything. Kick the dumpster or something. Make some sort of noise. We're open to you. Please let us know you're with us."

Suddenly music began to jingle. Startled out of their minds, both Vienna and Kim jumped. The coldness dissipated just as fast as it had occurred.

"My phone," Vienna said, laughing nervously when she recognized the song. She was getting a call on her cell phone. She fished the phone out of her jacket pocket and stared down at the number on the screen. It took her a second to register why the number seemed familiar. Then it dawned on her. The number belonged to Ryan.

Was this a sign from the ghost, she wondered, or just a coincidence.

She answered the phone.

Kim took the EMF detector from Vienna and did one more sweep of the alley.

"Hi," Vienna said, not really knowing what to say.

"She's gone," Kim said, returning to the dumpster, staring at the detector. "It's not even moving."

"Oh, that's my friend, Kim," Vienna explained. "Yeah, she's here visiting. Uh, huh. Sure. Okay. Tomorrow? Yeah, all right. Okay. Sounds good. Bye." Vienna pushed the little red phone icon making sure the call was disconnected before saying anything to Kim.

"Ryan?" Kim asked, her voice barely a whisper. She was still hoping the ghost would return.

"Yeah," Vienna said. "He asked me out. He heard your voice and I told him you were visiting. So he said he'd see if he has a friend he can set you up with. He wants us to go out tomorrow night."

"Awesome." Kim was still waving the EMF detector around hoping the needle would spike again.

"I don't know," Vienna said. "I just feel weird about this."

"Don't," Kim said. "You never know. He might be a really nice guy. Let's go back to the house and check out these EVPs. I bet we captured something."

"Yeah, right, nice guy," Vienna mumbled. Cold chills shot down her spine.

Tuesday, May 17
Chapter 11

Vienna rubbed her eyes with her fists. They burned from lack of sleep. No matter how hard she tried, she just couldn't fall asleep after hearing that eerie whisper on Kim's EVP recorder. After Kim had asked if the ghost was aware of the fact that she was dead it responded, "Help me." They were the same words that were written on the bathroom mirror.

At first, when they played back the EVP recording when they returned to the car, they hadn't noticed anything and were both kind of disappointed. The only thing they picked up on was what sounded like a bit of static or some kind of scratchy white noise in the background. In some ways it was sort of a letdown. And in other ways, Vienna was glad they hadn't gotten anything. Just being in the alley had rattled her nerves enough.

On the way home, they drove through a McDonalds and each ordered a large chocolate shake and extra large French fries as a pick-me-up. Kim was coping with disappointment and Vienna was coping with a bad case of the heebie jeebies. Either way, the fast food was a comfort food that they both needed.

When they returned to Vienna's Dad's house, Kim plugged the small EVP recorder into the thumb drive of Vienna's laptop. She downloaded a free computer software program that could be used to listen to and enhance recordings. It's the same kind of software that people used for cleaning up music recordings, audio recordings, and things of that nature.

Then it happened. Vienna still couldn't believe her ears. The whisper asking for help echoed in her mind. None of the questions that they had asked had been answered. But the ghost used whatever energy it could muster up, as Kim had explained, to get her point across to them. She needed their help.

Within the white noise, was a voice, a woman's voice that they hadn't noticed until running it through the software. Sarah had been very clear and precise. "Help me."

"How am I supposed to help someone who's dead?" Vienna asked. "It's impossible."

She wondered if she should do as Kim suggested and try to ask Jack for help. But she was too stubborn to do that. The thought of Jack and his smug, gorgeous, smile irked the heck out of her. She had no desire to admit to him that he was right, and that this might be her life's purpose. She knew she needed to somehow help this girl.

But just because she wanted to help her, didn't mean she'd be doing this for the rest of her life. As of right now, she had no intentions of dealing with the paranormal after she did what she could to help this girl.

That is, if she could help this girl. Then she would be done. No more nightmares, no more ghosts, and definitely no more contact with her spirit guide. Those things had no place in her world.

"Morning," Kim said while peeking around the doorjamb into Vienna's room. "How'd you sleep last night?"

Groggily, Vienna propped her head up. "I didn't."

"Me neither," Kim said. "I couldn't stop thinking of the EVP."

"Tell me about it."

"Bunny's already downstairs. Smells like she's making bacon and eggs."

"You're kidding." Vienna sat up and sniffed the air. The hickory smoked scent of bacon wafted into the bedroom causing Vienna's stomach to clench with hunger pangs. "I didn't know she cooked?"

"Thought I'd see if you're ready to venture downstairs with me."

"I am now," Vienna said, sniffing the air again. "I think I smell coffee, too."

Bunny was busily scrambling eggs while bacon was sizzling on the back burner. Poopsie was sitting on the tile floor staring up at her, sniffing the air, and licking his lips.

"Good morning!" Bunny chimed when she noticed Vienna and Kim entering the kitchen. "Help yourself to some coffee."

"Thanks." Vienna took down a couple of mugs from the cupboard next to the sink.

"Wow," Kim said. "That bacon smells incredible."

"It's my favorite," Bunny said. "I did a little shopping last night while you two were out. I thought a homemade breakfast would be nice."

"That's so sweet of you," Kim said. "Beautiful and can cook. Vienna's dad hit the jackpot."

Vienna did a mental eye roll. It wasn't that she didn't like Bunny, she just couldn't get used to the idea of Bunny and her father being a unit. Deep down inside she just always thought her parents would get back together. She knew it was silly. Here she was an adult and she still wanted her parents to be together as if she was a little child.

Bunny blushed. "Well, I wouldn't say that quite yet. You haven't tasted my cooking. So what did you guys do last night? Anything fun? Meet any cute boys?"

"We might have a double date tonight," Kim said.

Vienna threw Kim a look. She didn't want Bunny to know anything about Ryan or their paranormal investigation. She carried the coffee mugs over to the table and put one in front of Kim. Either Kim was ignoring Vienna's dirty look or didn't notice it because she continued the conversation.

"A double date? How fun!" Bunny squealed. "Is it with that guy Jack you've mentioned?"

"No," Vienna snapped.

"Jack? No," Kim smiled while shaking her head. "It's someone new."

"Tell me more," Bunny urged. "I love girl talk."

Vienna cut in before Kim said too much. "It's no one really. I'm not even interested in him."

"Oh," Bunny pouted, "that's too bad. Did you get suckered into saying yes? I hate it when that happens."

"That's exactly what happened," Vienna said, again giving Kim the evil eye. Kim was grinning.

Bunny grabbed some plates from the cupboard to the left of the stove and began serving breakfast. "You can always pretend to be sick," she suggested. "I've done that more than once."

"I don't think it'll work," Vienna said.

"Oh. He's one of those pushy guys." Bunny put a plate of bacon and eggs in front of Kim and handed the other to Vienna. She went back to prepare a plate for herself. "Well, PMS works. Guys never want to question PMS."

Kim laughed, "Nah, we're going. This Ryan guy might have a cute friend for me. And if he doesn't, well, Vienna can suddenly have bad cramps and we have to call it a night."

The rest of the day was pretty uneventful. The three of them lounged around the house, chatted, and spent the day relaxing. Kim painted her nails a dark purple to match a sequined top she planned to wear on their date. She even did her toenails. Vienna thought about painting her fingernails, but then thought of Ryan liking them and decided against it. She'd just leave them as is. She was only interested in his knowledge of Sarah. Or at least that's the name she was now calling the ghost.

After a long, lazy day, the last thing she wanted to do was go out. She'd rather continue her laziness into the night, lying on the couch, munching on chips, and watching movies. She'd even watch a sappy romance movie with Bunny. Listening to her sniffle and say every few minutes how sweet the movie was would be better than going out with Ryan.

Vienna checked her cell phone for the time. It was going on eight o'clock. She and Kim were supposed to

139

leave in ten minutes to meet Ryan and his friend Steve for dinner. Kim was adding last minute touches to her hair and makeup. Vienna was sitting at the foot of the bed, slipping on her socks, and tying the laces of her black sneakers. She refused to get all dressed up.

At Kim's request, she compromised and decided to wear something casual, but a little chic. She put on a pair of formfitting black jeans with a black leather belt, and was wearing a leopard print sleeveless top that belonged to Kim. The v-shaped neckline and the bottom of it were trimmed with black lace, and the silky satin material made it seem a little more than just a tank top.

"We've gotta go," Vienna said. "Otherwise we'll be late. It's ten 'til."

"Being late is fashionable," Kim said, exiting the bathroom in Vienna's room. She dropped her sparkly pearl pink lip gloss into her evening bag. "Okay, I'm ready. How do I look? Is my hair okay?" He patted her hair and pursed her glittery lips.

Kim's hair and makeup were perfect. She'd spent over an hour curling her gorgeous locks and another hour applying makeup.

A text message popped up on Vienna's phone. She touched the little envelope icon. "You'll never believe this," Vienna gaffed. "His friend cancelled. Can you believe it?"

"What? No way," Kim said. "You're kidding, right?"

"Nope. I kid you not."

"Men," Kim seethed. "And after all this work. It's not easy to do this." She grabbed a curly, blonde, streaked lock of hair and pulled. It bounced back into place.

"And get this... he wants to know if I'll still go out

with him. Yeah, right," Vienna said, shaking her head. "Forget it. What a creep."

Kim clutched Vienna's arm. "What about Sarah?"

"What about Sarah?" Vienna knew she shouldn't have told Kim that she thought the ghost girl's name was Sarah. Giving the ghost a name made her more real.

"She needs our help."

"So? What does that have to do with me going out with creepy Ryan? I'm sure we can find some other way to help her."

"Urrr!" Kim growled. "You just don't get it, do you? You only think he's creepy because he knows that guy from your dream. Or at least you think he knows the guy from your dream."

Vienna groaned. The last thing she wanted was a lecture.

"You know it's true," Kim said. "Is he cute?"

Vienna sighed.

"Come on," she urged. "Be truthful. Is he cute?"

Vienna shook her head. She really didn't want to answer. "He's okay, I guess. Not really my type."

Kim raised an eyebrow.

"Okay," Vienna admitted. "He's cute in a scruffy kind of way."

"Has he done anything to warrant creepy?"

Vienna gave Kim a look.

"Besides being a friend to the murderer in your dream…"

"No, I guess not." Vienna rolled her shoulders back. She didn't like being cornered and Kim was putting her on the defensive. "But you can't tell me it's not weird. I mean, come on."

"They were only coworkers," Kim argued while pacing the room. "Not best friends. Right?"

"And your point is?"

"My point is that we're at a dead end. Sarah needs our help. She wouldn't be entering your dreams if she didn't need you. And last night, she asked us on the recorder to help her. We need to do something. You, yourself, asked what you can do to help a ghost. Well, this might be it."

Vienna groaned. She knew she was right. Kim plopped down next to her.

"Come on. You can't deny it. You heard her ask for our help just like I did. We can't ignore that. And Ryan's our only lead. He could at least give us the name of his coworker. Right now all we got is a first name. If that's even the right name. You said that Goldie guy seemed to make Ryan nervous. He may have been lying."

"I'm sure Goldie makes a lot of men nervous. He's pretty straight forward and he put Ryan on the spot," she answered. "But I don't think he was lying."

Vienna's mind drifted back to the EVP they got last night. She could still hear the eerie whisper of Sarah's voice echo in her head asking for help. She knew Kim was right. They had to do something to help her, but what? How do you help a dead person? She heaved a sigh, "And once we get the guy's name, then what do we do?"

"I don't know. I guess we can give it to the police to investigate. We can leave an anonymous tip or something."

Vienna nodded. She and Kim both knew that they couldn't tell the truth of how they knew this information. Who would believe that a ghost came to them for help?

She knew she wouldn't believe it if someone else told her that story. She'd wonder if that person was off their rocker.

"Do you think if we get the guy's name and give it to the police that Sarah would be happy?" Vienna asked. "Do you think that's the help she wants?"

Kim mulled this over and shrugged. "I don't know, but it's worth a try. If I was murdered, I'd want the person that did it to me to be caught and brought to justice. And I'd haunt his sorry butt just to get even. I'd literally scare the pee out of him every chance I got."

Vienna knew Kim would have no qualms about haunting the heck out of someone that had wronged her. Once she had a boyfriend cheat on her and she made his life a living hell. After a while Vienna began to feel sorry for the poor guy, even though he was a first class jerk. He had no idea who he was messing with.

Out of the blue, a thought just occurred to her that might lead to more information on this supposed guy that they felt murdered Sarah. "Why don't we call that computer place that the murderer worked for and try to get a last name?"

"Do you really think they'd just give us information on an employee who used to work there that we think is named Nathan? I highly doubt it. They might give us a last name if we're lucky, but they won't answer any questions about a woman he might have been dating."

"No, guess not," Vienna said. Her cell phone vibrated again. She glanced at the screen. Ryan had sent another text. "He said he still has dinner reservations for us and can come pick me up if I want."

"Do it," Kim urged. "Do it for Sarah."

Vienna sent a text message back with her dad's address. "I feel uneasy about this."

"Don't," Kim said, taking Vienna's hand and patting it. "You just haven't been on a date in a long time. It's understandable since your breakup with Brandon. I know how much you wanted it to work out."

Vienna's eyes filled with tears. Maybe Kim was right. Maybe her fear of going out with Ryan mainly stemmed from her painful breakup with Brandon. She'd gone on a few blind dates since their relationship ended but they didn't go so well either. It's no wonder she was gun shy.

"It's okay," Kim said. "Even if you're not attracted to this guy, you'll still have a good time going out and being pampered a bit. Trust me."

Vienna sighed. "Okay."

They sat in silence for a moment. Kim tilted her head to the side and frowned. Vienna could tell she was concerned for her. "You okay?"

"Yeah, I'm fine. Maybe this date is what I need."

"That's the spirit." Kim grinned. "You'll have a good time. I just know it."

"I've got an idea though," Vienna said, her mood brightening. "While I'm pumping Ryan for info you can call the computer company that he works for."

"They're not going to give me information. We just talked about…"

"No, no, no." Vienna put her hand up to silence Kim so she could finish her thought. "I know that. Just call and say you're having computer problems. Fake some problems with my laptop to get someone out here."

"I can do that," Kim said, proudly. "What should I say is the matter with it?"

"Um… won't turn on or something. Tell them you've tried everything and you really need someone to look at it tonight. Tell them you're desperate. I'll give you my credit card to use."

"What's the name of the company?"

"I'm not sure. So you'll have to do some research. Maybe Bunny knows the name. If not, I'm sure you can look it up online or in the phone book. It's the one with the cars that look like bugs. You know, they're supposed to be computer virus bugs."

"Oh, yeah, I've seen those. Gotcha. Bugs. A play on words. Cute."

Just then the doorbell rang. "Guess he lives pretty close," Kim said. "He's already here."

"Yeah. Or maybe he's coming from work." Vienna scooped up her purse from the bed. "Here goes nothing. Wish me luck."

Kim put her hand on Vienna's shoulder. "Don't worry. You'll have fun. Trust me."

"Yeah, sure," Vienna said, forcing a smile to appease Kim just as Bunny called her from downstairs.

***

The restaurant was beautiful. It wasn't one that Vienna had ever been to before. She'd passed it many times while driving down highway 111 over the years and had always been curious as to what it would be like on the inside. Now she knew.

Shiny black lacquered rectangular tables and black matching wooden chairs with high backs and red upholstered seats were arranged nicely throughout the building lining the natural looking stone walls. A long stainless steel sushi bar sat to the far left of the restaurant with a lower polished black counter. Numerous customers were seated at the bar chatting, laughing and eating. To the right of the restaurant, small long windows were carved into the stone near the ceiling. During daylight hours they'd filter in just enough light giving the restaurant a romantic skylight ambience. Since the restaurant was built into the side of a rocky hill, partially underground, Vienna thought it was really neat that the windows were actually ground level when standing outside the building.

Vienna was hoping they'd be seated at the sushi bar. Sitting with a bunch of other people would make her dinner date a lot less uncomfortable. But to her dismay, Ryan had arranged ahead of time, for the two of them to have a small table tucked away in a dark romantic corner. She sat down across from him and tried really hard not to be too obvious about the fact that she was trembling inside with nerves.

Regardless, of her anxious state, she had to admit in the dim lighting, Ryan who was sporting a lopsided grin, was sort of cute. His green eyes seemed to glow brightly in contrast to his dark hair. And tonight he was smartly dressed in a white polo shirt and tan slacks. His face was no longer scruffy like she had remembered from that night a Goldie's. His chin and jaw line were now clean-shaven and completely smooth.

Besides just cleaning himself up to impress Vienna, Ryan had even gone as far as pulling out a chair for her to sit down at the table. She could tell he was trying really hard to be a gentleman. When he'd picked her up for their date, he handed her a single red rose which she'd left with Bunny to put in some water.

"I'm sorry my friend backed out," Ryan said, twisting

a gold class ring with a deep red stone on the middle finger of his right hand.

"That's okay," Vienna said. "It happens." She picked up her glass of water and took a sip. She was still feeling a bit awkward.

"Is she upset?" he asked, looking up from his ring.

"Kim?" Vienna put her glass down. "No. She's fine. No big deal."

Vienna could feel the intensity of Ryan's stare. His green eyes seemed to bore right into her. He was taking in every detail of her appearance. She suddenly felt very self-conscious. She reached up and tucked her dark shoulder length hair behind her ears.

"I was afraid you'd back out," he said, still raking his eyes over her.

Vienna unconsciously slipped off her glasses and wiped the lenses with the bottom of her shirt. She didn't know how to respond to his comment.

"Am I making you nervous?" he asked, his voice almost a whisper. "I don't mean to. I want you to feel comfortable with me."

"Have you had time to look over the menu?" asked a smiling woman in a Japanese kimono. Her silky black hair was twisted in a bun and held in place by two decorative chopsticks.

"No," Vienna said, slipping her glasses back on to have a look at the menu. "Not yet."

"We're ready," Ryan said. He promptly ordered dinner for the two of them. The woman scribbled on her notepad and asked a few questions regarding the soup and appetizers then headed in the direction of the kitchen.

Vienna wanted to say something to Ryan about

ordering for her without asking what she liked first, but instead bit her tongue. She didn't want to cause a scene and she really didn't know anything about Sushi, fish, or Japanese food. The menu might as well have been written in Japanese because she'd felt completely lost when looking over the selection. Maybe she was being too hard on Ryan. He was probably just trying to impress her with his knowledge of Japanese cuisine.

"How long is your friend visiting for?" he asked, as soon as the waitress had left the table.

"Oh, we're both flying home on Monday morning."

"Both?" He lifted a thick dark eyebrow. "What do you mean, both?"

"Oh." Vienna was caught by surprise. She forgot that he hadn't known that she herself was just visiting. "I don't live here in the desert. My dad has a house here."

"I see," he said, very calmly. "Do you visit often?"

"From time to time," she said. "I can visit whenever I want."

"Where's home?"

"Sacramento. I go to college there, Sac state."

"So," he said, eyes unblinking, "us meeting at Goldie's was fate."

Just then the waitress showed up with two white ceramic bowls of steaming soup. She placed a bowl in front of each of them. When she left, Vienna excused herself to freshen up in the restroom. She made up some sort of nonsense about not being able to eat until her hands were washed.

Once secured in a stall, she dug her cell phone out of her purse and sent a text message to Kim with the name of the restaurant she was at. As soon as the soup had arrived, an urgent thought had come to her out of nowhere, and she needed to make sure someone knew where she was.

Now that the text had been sent, the urgency of the matter diminished. She could relax a little and try to enjoy dinner.

***

After Ryan had picked up Vienna for their date, Bunny asked Kim if she'd like to go see a movie or something. But Kim knew she had some work to do and made up an excuse as to why she needed to stay there at the house. She told Bunny that she promised Vienna she'd have someone look at her laptop because it was having problems. To her surprise, Bunny didn't question her too much about it.

"We could go drop it off somewhere on the way to the movies," Bunny offered.

"No, um…" Kim pursed her lips while trying to find an excuse as to why that wouldn't work. "Vienna mentioned a place that's supposed to be really good and they do house calls."

"Oh." Bunny frowned.

Kim knew her excuse sounded pretty lame so she tried to elaborate. "I mean, well, you know when you use a place that's really good, you continue to use them? Kinda like when you find a good beautician. You don't want to use someone else because you want to make sure your hair looks good. It's the same kind of thing. I think Vienna just wants to make sure they do a good job and fix her computer. She swears that this company is the best."

Bunny smiled and nodded. Kim had obviously gotten her point across. If she could help it, Bunny tried to use the same beautician for that very reason. She held a finger in the air. "I've got an idea," she said. "How about we order in and rent a movie?"

"That would be great," Kim agreed. "I'm starved."

"Pizza?"

"Sounds awesome," Kim said as Bunny left the living room and headed to the kitchen. Kim followed, passing the table to the counter by the sliding glass door leading to the backyard. "This may sound weird, but do you by any chance know the name of the computer place that has the cars that look like bugs? I can't remember."

Picking up the phone, Bunny hesitated and tapped her bottom lip with her index finger. "I know which one you're talking about. I just can't think of the name." She opened a cabinet below the countertop where the phone was stationed and pulled out the Yellow Pages. "I bet they're in here."

"Thanks." Kim spread open the book on the table and began flipping through the pages.

"Do you mind a vegetarian pizza with rice crust? I'm in the mood for something healthy."

"Sure, whatever you want. I'm not picky." Kim turned the pages until she came to the C's.

"How about a scary movie?" Bunny asked. "I'm usually too chicken to watch something scary, but I just remembered that I saw a preview for a movie on pay per view that looked really good. It's also a love story. I'm a sucker for romance."

"Sure. Okay," Kim said. "Sounds good to me." With her finger pressed to the page, she skimmed down the list of computer repair ads. She hoped to find an advertisement with a photo of the cars that looked like bugs. Two pages in, she struck gold. A car with big antennas and googly eyes was on the page in full vibrant color.

Bunny was on the line, putting in their pizza order when Kim snuck out of the room with the phone book tucked under her arm. When she reached her room, she took out her cell phone to dial the computer shop. But before she called, she received Vienna's text message. Nothing was mentioned about the date or how things were going. Only the name of the restaurant they were at.

Kim texted back, "Found the bug place. About to make a call. Hope you're having fun."

She sent the text and dialed the computer store. After what seemed like an eternity of waiting on hold and listening to elevator music, Kim got a real live person.

"Hi, yes, I'd like someone to come and look at my computer tonight. What? No, I don't care how much it costs, it's urgent… No, it has to be tonight… I can't wait a couple of days… It's having a problem starting up… Yes, I'll hold."

Chapter 12

Dinner had been fantastic. Vienna was so relieved that Jack, her supposed spirit guide was still MIA, missing in action. She bet that he'd find a way to totally ruin her night if he was still around. It bugged her to no end that Jack had entered her mind when she was having such a good time. Urr! He was still managing to irk her even when he wasn't in her life. Why was she even thinking about him? She pushed his handsome, grinning face from her thoughts and smiled across the table at Ryan. He returned the smile.

Vienna was kicking herself for having been so nervous around Ryan. They'd actually been having a really good time. They'd even shared a few stupid jokes and talked a lot about art.

Ryan's vast knowledge of art history had been surprising. Even though Vienna was an artist, she new very little about the history portion of it. Most of her time was spent in the studio either painting or sculpting. She preferred hands on, over studying the history. But it was refreshing to meet someone who was interested in her artistry. He even asked questions about what she prefers to paint and what her favorite colors were.

She knew she should've used this time more wisely by asking questions about Sarah, and about Ryan's coworker, Nathan. She really wanted to ask if he knew whether or not Sarah and Nathan had known each other before that fateful night. She had so many important questions that kept nagging at her, but she didn't want to ruin their date by bringing up something so dismal and depressing. They were having such a good time.

Besides, he'd totally think she was some crazy psycho if she confided in him about her dream. Even when running the scenario through her head, she sounded crazy.

Vienna decided to hold onto her questions for a little while longer. She wanted to get to know Ryan a bit more before bombarding him with things about stuff she didn't even know how to bring up.

After they finished dinner, Vienna excused herself to use the restroom. She locked herself into the same stall and quickly sent a text message over to Kim.

"Dinner was great. Having dessert then I'll be back. Won't stay out late. Thanks for making me go."

Kim responded immediately, "Having computer looked at. Glad dinner went well. See you soon. Hopefully with info and juicy gossip!!!"

Vienna headed back to the table. Ryan's intense green eyes were watching her. To her surprise, he had ordered a bottle of red wine to go with dessert. Vienna smiled and took a sip from the glass he presented to her.

***

"Oh, silly me," Kim giggled. "You mean to tell me that the laptop needs a battery? I had no idea."

"Or plugged in." The young man, who looked barely eighteen, blushed.

"I feel so stupid." Kim pushed her fingers to her forehead.

"Don't worry. It happens more often than you think."

"It's my friend's computer and I just couldn't get it to work. I guess I panicked thinking I broke it or something."

"It's okay."

"I really didn't know I could just plug it in."

Running his hand through his short brown hair the computer repair man laughed, "Yeah, laptops can be plugged in."

"That's good to know," Kim said. "I won't be making that mistake again. I should've just called my friend, but she's on a date and I didn't want to bother her. But I really needed to go online to do some school work and I remembered her mentioning that she used your company to fix her computer before."

"Oh, okay." He smiled, his cheeks were still red. "Well, I don't think there's much more I can do here since you're up and running."

Kim knew she needed to do something to stall the computer guy. She couldn't let him leave without asking a few questions about Nathan. Since she was all out of stupid computer questions, she decided to do what she knew how to do best. Flirt. She fluttered her eyelashes and began to twirl a clump of her blonde hair to get his attention.

"The guy that usually works on my friend's computer... I can't remember what his name is," Kim said in her most girly tone of voice. She leaned in and played with the computer guy's name tag, attached to his shirt. "Um, Chad," she read his name and provocatively touched his chest as if feeling his muscles, "maybe you'll know his name."

Chad cleared his throat as if searching for his voice. He squeaked, "Well, there are several of us." He cleared his throat again. "So I'm not sure…"

Kim interrupted him, "I think he stopped working there recently. Or at least that's what I've been told."

"Oh, you're probably thinking of Nathan Cooper."

"Nathan Cooper," Kim said excitedly. "Yes, I think that's the guy she mentioned. Does he have dark hair and is about this tall?" She put her hand up above her head to emphasize that he was quite tall.

"Yeah, could be him," Chad said, still blushing. "Well, I'd better get back to the store." He turned to leave the room.

"Wait," Kim said, putting her hand on his shoulder, stopping him. "I haven't paid yet. I remember Vienna saying that Nathan, her usual computer guy, gives discounts."

"No charge," Chad's voice cracked. He reached up and tugged at the collar of his forest green shirt as if the temperature in the room had just raised a notch. His face grew even redder at Kim's constant touch. She still had her hand on his shoulder, holding him there.

"No charge?" Kim pushed her way in front of Chad blocking him from leaving the bedroom. "Are you sure? You had to waste your time driving all the way over here. What about gas money?"

"It's a company car. Besides, I don't feel right

charging you for an unplugged laptop." He tried to take a step forward, but Kim didn't move.

"You are so sweet!" she gushed, tilting her head to the side while tossing her long blonde hair over her shoulder.

"Thanks," he said, trying again to get around her. They did a little dance. Kim side stepped him twice.

"I just have one more question before you go," she said, holding up her index finger for emphasis.

Chad looked down at his watch. "Okay."

"It's about Nathan."

Chad's smile vanished. "Okay. What about him?"

"My friend has this huge crush on him and I was just wondering if he had a girlfriend. She'd heard through the grapevine that he was seeing a girl named, Sarah. Is that true?"

Chad shrugged. "I really don't know. The guy was kind of a player. He was always bragging about different girls he was with."

"Oh," Kim said, feeling deflated. She was hoping he'd have some information about Sarah. A last name would've been more than helpful. Oh well. At least she knew Nathan's last name. "So, you've never heard Nathan mention a girl named Sarah?"

"Uh, no, sorry," Chad said, shaking his head. "The guy was kind of a jerk. I didn't talk to him much."

"That bad, huh?"

"Yeah. And get this, he just stopped coming into work a couple weeks ago. The rest of us have been trying to pick up the slack ever since. Can you believe it? The stupid jerk quit without even giving notice. I've been working a lot of double shifts lately."

"Oh," Kim said, "yeah, that's pretty bad. Guess it's a good thing my friend never went out with him."

"Yeah," Chad said. "He's the total opposite of me." Chad averted his eyes after making that comment. So did Kim. She wondered if he said that because he was interested in her. Maybe he wanted her to know that he wasn't a jerk like Nathan.

"I'd better let you go." Kim moved out of his way. "I know you're in a hurry."

"Yeah," he said, glancing at his watch again. "We're short handed at the shop."

Kim followed him down the stairs to the front door to see him out. "Thanks again for your help."

"No problem," Chad said, "just remember to plug the laptop in next time."

Kim could feel her cheeks burning. It was her turn to feel embarrassed. "Uh, yeah. I'll keep that in mind. Thanks."

***

Feeling quite comfortable after a glass of red wine, and a bowl of green tea ice cream, Vienna decided to ask Ryan about Nathan.

Ryan added more wine to Vienna's glass. "What about him?"

"I don't know," she said, not really wanting to explain about Sarah being the focus of her nightmares. Instead, she focused on Goldie. "Goldie had mentioned him when we met at the club."

Ryan didn't say anything. His green eyes stared intently into Vienna's. Suddenly she felt very strange and vulnerable, almost as if she was sitting there naked, exposed, for the entire world to see.

Crossing her arms over her chest, almost like a shield or blanket to protect herself, Vienna continued, "I was just looking for something to talk about. If you don't want to talk about it, we can change the subject."

"Ah," Ryan said, but didn't elaborate. He leaned back in his chair and sat in silence, watching the people sitting across the room from them.

Vienna wondered if she'd somehow struck a nerve asking about Nathan. But why would that bother him? Maybe she should just tell him the truth and go from there. She blinked hard a couple of times. Her eyes were having a hard time focusing on Ryan's face. His mouth was pulled tight and his eyes were dark and blurry. She blinked hard again. Ryan had one big eye smack in the middle of his forehead. She closed her eyes and rubbed beneath them while trying not to smear her black eyeliner. She opened her eyes and straightened her glasses. Now his eyes were back to normal.

The only explanation was that the wine seemed to have gone straight to her head. She was seeing things. Obviously sushi wasn't much of a meal when it came to soaking up alcohol. Her vision was still a bit off. She blinked hard again and reached for the water glass.

Water should help, she thought. She gulped it down wishing she had another glass. Her mouth felt dry and her tongue swollen.

"The reason I brought up Nathan," Vienna began to explain, her words slurring. "That's his name, right? Nathan. That's what I remember you saying. Nathan."

Ryan raised a dark eyebrow in response. His voice was calm, "Yes, Nathan."

"The reason…" Vienna pressed her index and middle

finger to her forehead to try to steady her thoughts. "The reason I brought him up is because of this dream I've had." Out of nowhere, she began to giggle nervously. "I know I'm going to sound crazy. It's so ridiculous sounding... oh boy, that wine is strong..."

"You feeling okay?" Ryan asked, reaching across the table and putting his hand on hers.

"Uh, yeah," Vienna said, still working on keeping her thoughts straight. Her mind wanted to drift. "I think I just need some more water. I'm really thirsty." She reached for her empty glass and frowned. Even the ice was gone. She didn't remember chewing the ice, but she must have.

Ryan slid his glass across the table. "Have mine."

"Thanks." Taking a sip, she sighed, "This is so weird. My mouth is so dry. Wow. Um, what was I saying?"

"About Nathan and a dream," he prompted.

"Oh, yeah, what I'm trying to say is... I know this sounds crazy, but I dreamt that your friend, Nathan, killed this girl named Sarah." For no apparent reason, Vienna giggled again. "Nuts, huh?"

"Coworker," Ryan corrected. "Not friend."

"Oh, yes, coworker." Vienna picked up Ryan's glass and sipped more water. At first the iciness of the liquid felt comforting in her stomach, but it didn't last long. Her head was beginning to spin out of control and nausea was taking over. "Oh, God." Vienna slapped her hand over her mouth. Through her fingers she moaned, "This is so embarrassing. I'm feeling pretty sick. I think I'm going to throw up."

Ryan hopped up from his seat. "Let me get the bill and we'll go out for some fresh air."

"Okay, thanks."

Wednesday, May 18
Chapter 13

With her fists, Kim rubbed her eyes as she slowly came to. A bit disoriented, it took her a second or two to remember where she was. Across the room she could see Bunny sound asleep in the recliner with Poopsie curled up on her legs.

The TV was still on. Sitting up on the couch, stretching, Kim stared at the movie previews. She and Bunny had fallen asleep during the movie. The last thing she remembered was a pack of zombies chasing a gorgeous hunk of a man, and beautiful golden haired woman with way too much makeup on and a body to kill for, through an abandoned town, trying to suck their brains. It was a typical zombie movie, with state of the art graphics, and a massive love affair that bloomed between the two main characters.

Kim wasn't sure she'd be in the mood for a romantic relationship no matter how gorgeous the guy was while having brain eating zombies on her tail, but that was just her opinion. The movie did well in the theatre, so people must've liked it. She had found it somewhat entertaining, but not enough to keep her from falling asleep.

"Bunny." Kim gently shook her awake. Poopsie stood up and arched his back, stretching. "Bunny, we fell asleep. Bunny."

"Hmmm," Bunny mumbled, trying to open her eyes. "What?"

"We fell asleep," Kim repeated.

"Oh," she said. "Okay." In a daze, Bunny stood up and stumbled up the stairs to her room. Poopsie followed, his little claws clicking on the tile and dog tags jingling from his collar.

Kim turned off the TV and began to switch off the lights when it dawned on her that she hadn't heard from Vienna. Glancing at her watch, she frowned. It was twenty minutes past midnight. The last text she'd received was around 9:45 when Vienna said she'd be home after dessert.

Kim scooped up her cell phone from the floor. It had fallen off the couch some time during the movie. She checked for new text messages, but hadn't received any.

Maybe Vienna's date is going better than expected, Kim thought.

She pushed the little button on the top of her phone, switching it off. In the past, she'd missed several text messages that had somehow gotten held up in cyberspace somewhere then after shutting off her phone and rebooting it, old text messages and emails came through. She hoped that was the case tonight. Maybe a text from Vienna saying that she decided to stay out late got held up.

Kim made her way upstairs to Vienna's room while waiting for her phone to reboot. She wondered if maybe

Vienna had come home already and went straight to bed. But she had a hard time believing that Vienna would leave her and Bunny sleeping in front of the TV. Even if she didn't want to disturb them, Kim knew that Vienna would switch off the television and lights and cover them with blankets. She was always thoughtful about things like that.

Kim cracked open the door to Vienna's room and peeked in. The light from the hall spilled into the bedroom and across the empty bed. Kim's stomach turned.

Where was Vienna?

She looked down at her phone that finished its reboot. No new messages.

***

"Wake up!" Jack urged. Even in an unconscious state, Vienna was being stubborn and blocking him out. "Come on, Vienna, wake up!"

Standing next to the bed, Jack focused on rounding up his energy to make his hands corporeal. He was having a hard time due to the dryness of the desert air. Pulling every bit of moisture from the night, he concentrated on his hands. His fingertips tingled as they became solid.

"Vienna," he said telepathically, gripping her shoulders, shaking her. He wanted her to wake up, but he didn't want her to be startled. "Wake up, Vienna." He shook her some more.

Vienna muttered something in her sleep and rolled over. Jack released his energy that was making his hands substantial. Instead, he focused it elsewhere. He put his hand to Vienna's temple, leaned in so that his forehead was virtually touching hers and melted his mind into hers.

"Jack?" she asked. Vienna was sitting alone at a small

163

table, sipping tea. She was wearing a flowered sundress and her hair was pulled up in a bun. Little ringlets of hair had come loose at the sides and delicately framed her face. "I was wondering when you'd arrive? You're late for tea."

Jack took in his surroundings. They were in what seemed to be an English cottage in the late 1800s. The room was small, but very ornate and the walls were painted a brick red. A wooden curio-cabinet filled with china was against the wall behind Vienna. An oil painting of the English countryside with brilliant rolling green hills was next to it. Just beneath was an extra chair for the table. His eyes followed the white crown molding around the ceiling. The more he studied the room, the more things seemed to keep appearing. More paintings, more candle holders, more shelves. Suddenly a fireplace formed out of nowhere. "Vienna," he said. "I need to talk to you. It's important."

"Have some tea," Vienna said. A white teacup, hand painted with dainty pink roses around the rim, magically appeared in front of Jack. Vienna lifted the matching porcelain teapot and poured him a cup. "Would you like some cream and sugar?"

"Where are we?" Jack asked.

Vienna looked around the small dining room. "In my home, of course. Where else would we be?"

"Oh, yes," he said. "Of course."

"You like it?" she asked. "I decorated it myself. Here, have a biscuit. You must be famished."

"It's very nice. Cozy." Jack took a biscuit from the plate that Vienna conjured up out of thin air. "Thank you."

"I love it here," Vienna said. "So peaceful. I had a

really good life here, you know. Oh, that reminds me, you should see my garden. I have the most beautiful flowers. I planted them all myself." A blue and white ceramic vase of freshly cut white and yellow daisies appeared as a center piece on the table.

"Maybe another time." Jack smiled warmly at her. "Vienna, I need to talk to you about something important. It's extremely serious. I need you to listen to me."

"Not now. Can't it wait," she said, hastily. "It's so nice here."

"No," Jack said, gently. "It can't wait. You're in danger."

Vienna laughed then covered her mouth with a white dainty, hand-embroidered napkin. She dabbed at the corners of her lips. "I'm not in any danger. That's the silliest thing I've ever heard. Why do you always want to spoil my fun?"

"Vienna," Jack said, seriously. "You're dreaming." He held out his hand and motioned for her to take a look around the room. "None of this is real. I'm here to wake you up."

Vienna followed his hand and took in the warmness of the room and thought about things for a moment. "But I like it here," she said. "I don't want to wake up."

"You need to."

Again she glanced around the room. She leaned in and whispered as if telling him a secret, "I lived here once. It was a long time ago. I've made a few improvements since then. Some things I can't live without." A brand new zebra striped iPod player materialized on the table next to the plate of biscuits.

Jack nodded. "Yes, but you don't live here anymore.

It's fine to visit, but now you're needed in your current time. You need to wake up."

"What if I don't want to?"

"You need to. It's urgent."

"Oh, my, do you smell that?" Vienna's eyes grew large. She quickly hopped up from her chair almost knocking it over. "Please, excuse me. I completely forgot my bread. Did you know that I bake fresh bread? They say it's the best in the village."

"Vienna?" Jack stood up. He could smell something burning. Vienna fled through a doorway that led to the kitchen. Jack tried to follow, but she vanished. He stared into the room she'd entered, but could see nothing. The room he was standing in dissolved all around him until he was standing alone in a white, blank place. No floor, no ceiling, no walls, nothing. It all disappeared. Vienna had blocked him out.

Jack pressed his eyes closed. And when he opened them, he found himself back in the dark bedroom. His forehead was hovering just above Vienna's. He lifted up, removing his thoughts and energy that had been mingling with hers. He took in the colors of her aura and then let his eyes linger for a while on the softness of her face and then the slight curve of her chin. He felt an attachment unlike one that he was accustomed to on the other side. It had been a long time since he'd had these kinds of feelings. It had been over a century since he'd lived on the physical plane. And this attachment he was feeling was a human attachment, one that manifested within a physical body. A deep loving ache burned within his soul. He tried to push the feelings away. He needed to keep his mind clear and not mottled with human emotion. He needed to help

Vienna.

Jack stroked the soft skin of Vienna's cheek with invisible fingers, lightly tickling her with his energy. She was still sound asleep, deeply engaged in her dream. His energy waves seemed to make no difference in her state of being. Nothing he could do would wake her. His attempts were useless.

Noticing the flickering light for the first time, he realized that candles had been strategically placed around the room while he'd been visiting Vienna's dream.

Three burning candles were on the bedside table, three candles evenly spaced on the dresser beneath the window, and three candles on the cement floor in the far corner. The burning wicks were casting a warm glow within the room.

Jack wondered how much time had ticked by while he was trying to reach Vienna. Time was tricky to measure unless you were bound to the human realm. He surmised that enough of it had to have gone by in order for Ryan to have entered the room and to have set up and lit the candles. The candles seemed to have been placed in some sort of thoughtful order. They weren't just randomly clumped. And each was in a group of three.

Jack roamed the room. He didn't recall seeing any unlit candles before his dreamscape with Vienna. But then again, his mind was on reaching her, not the décor of the room.

Vienna looked so peaceful lying there. He began to feel another human emotion coming over him. Worry. He'd been taking human form too often.

Jack tried again to touch her face. She responded by rolling over onto her side, and cuddling up to a ratty old pillow. He watched Vienna sleep for a moment; her breathing was slow and deep. That was when he realized her glasses were missing. She wasn't wearing them. He found them on the small table next to the bed. Ryan must've removed them when he came in to light the candles because Vienna still had them on when Jack first arrived.

Knowing that he couldn't rouse Vienna, and that he was wasting valuable time, Jack decided he'd have to do something rash. He'd have to act quickly. There was no telling what Ryan had planned for her, and exactly how long he planned to wait before doing it. Vienna was in terrible danger. He could feel the negative energy, which had seeped out of Ryan, radiating throughout the room. He needed to do something and quick.

"Vienna," Jack whispered into her ear. "I'll be back soon with help." He pulled his energy into his fingertips and lovingly smoothed her hair away from her face.

Kim was the first thought that came to his mind. He needed to contact Kim.

***

Kim lay in bed staring at the ceiling making shapes out of the texture in the moonlight. Her mind was restless because she didn't know what to do about Vienna. She had sent a text message to Vienna's cell phone well over an hour ago checking in on her, but had received no response. Then she tried calling and her phone went straight to voice mail. The only explanations that didn't send her into a panic was that Vienna was having such a good time that she hadn't checked her phone or that the battery had died, and because of her having such a great date she didn't notice. But she didn't believe either one of them to be true.

Kim rolled over and grabbed her cell phone from the nightstand. Still no messages.

She wondered if she should wake Bunny. Maybe Bunny would know what to do. She wanted to call the police, but she knew that Vienna hadn't been missing for a long enough time. And what if she did call the police and put in a report and then Vienna showed up at home a few moments later.

Kim frowned at her phone. She needed to do something. Lying in bed thinking about Vienna wasn't helping any. There had to be something she could do.

Just then Kim's phone chimed. She received a text message from an unknown source. Kim touched the envelop icon, opening it.

"Vienna's in trouble. Jack."

Kim bolted out of bed. Trembling, she switched on the light switch and looked around the empty room.

"Jack," she said. "Jack, are you here with me? Give me some sort of sign."

The lamp on the nightstand flickered.

"Okay. You're here. I wish I could see you."

Jack summoned up energy from the lamp causing it to flicker again. He conjured up just enough to make himself visible, yet transparent.

"Oh, my God." Kim placed her hand to her racing heart. "I can see you."

The bedside light flashed in response.

"Where's Vienna? What can I do?"

"She's in trouble," Jack answered, his voice barely a whisper. Kim had to concentrate to understand him. "She's with Ryan. She's been drugged. I can't wake her."

"What's the address?" Kim grabbed her black leather jacket from the closet and a pair of sneakers and slipped them on.

"I'll take you there."

"Should I call the police?"

"If the police show up, he might kill her out of panic. He's not stable."

"Oh my God, what are we going to do?"

"Get her out of there."

"Good plan." Kim grabbed the key to the rental car that Vienna had left with her in case she had needed it. "Let's go."

***

Vienna rubbed her eyes. Her mind was groggy and her body felt weighted down and hard to move. She forced her eyes to open. The lids were heavy and burned as if rubbed raw with sandpaper. An odd flickering light caught her attention. Candles were everywhere.

Candles? Vienna wondered. Where am I?

She tried again to get her body to move. It didn't want to. Her brain seemed both sluggish and incompliant at getting her limbs to move.

Struggling to sit up, Vienna forced down an unexpected wave of nausea. There was a burning sensation deep in the pit of her stomach. Her head was spinning out of control and the room was blurry. She couldn't seem to focus on anything and she wanted to panic. And the flickering of candlelight bouncing off the walls wasn't helping the situation any.

Vienna reached up and touched her face and realized she wasn't wearing her glasses. If she could see better, she might be able to focus her thoughts and figure out where the heck she was.

Swinging her legs off the bed, she closed her eyes and sat still for a moment and listened. She couldn't hear anything. Searching her memory, she tried to remember what had last happened to her.

"Dinner with Ryan," she whispered. He had walked her out to his truck and said he'd take care of her because she'd had too much to drink. She vaguely remembered pressing her cheek against the window because the coolness of the glass helped to keep her from throwing up. She must've fallen asleep.

Squinting, she looked around the room. He obviously hadn't taken her home. Well, not to her home, anyway. This had to be Ryan's room. Vienna felt the top of a small wooden table next to the bed that was in place of a nightstand. To her relief her glasses were there. Slipping them on, she felt a little better. Now she could see.

Vienna walked over to the bedroom door. She turned the knob, but the door wouldn't budge. That wasn't what she'd expected. She figured that Ryan just laid her down to sleep off the alcohol. But if that was the case, why was the door locked? She tried the knob again. The doorknob turned, but the door wouldn't open.

"What the...?"

Suddenly alert and nausea gone, Vienna turned the knob and leaned against the door with the full weight of her body in case it was just stuck. She knew that temperature changes could make wooden doors swell, especially in old houses. And from what she could tell by the state of this room, it seemed pretty old and run down. Paint was peeling off the walls and there was no carpet.

Only a dirt covered cement slab. So she wouldn't be at all surprised if that was the case. Swollen doors.

Leaning into the door, her heart sunk. Still no movement.

A thought struck her; Ryan had a padlock on the other side of the door securing her in this room. How she knew this, she wasn't sure, but she could envision the lock in her mind. It was silver and small. There was a rusted latch bolted to the wall and the door. It had been there for a long time. It was originally put on by the previous owner. He used to keep his wife locked in here.

Bad things had happened in this room prior to Ryan finding it. She felt that the dark energy in this building was helping to fuel Ryan's sickness. It was empowering the evil within him.

Vienna wanted to panic. Ryan had locked her in. She was his prisoner. She wasn't imagining things. This wasn't a dream. This was real and this was truly happening.

A couple of swift hard kicks would break the hold on the door. But it would also alert Ryan.

Running to the window that was over the dresser, Vienna yanked open the thick drapes and choked on a billow of powdery desert dust. The window was boarded up with a thick sheet of plywood.

Where the hell was she? She couldn't see out. Should she start screaming for help and bang on the walls? Would someone besides Ryan hear her? Or would he be the only one. That would make him angry. His bright green eyes flashed in her mind. He was going to hurt her.

What was she going to do? An even worse thought occurred to her; what was he going to do?

Chapter 14

Dark, with only the light of the moon to guide them, Kim switched off the headlights and crept down the dirt road. Jack told her they were getting close. And she didn't want to alert Ryan of their arrival.

The drive had felt like it took an eternity. They were a good forty five miles away from Vienna's father's house. He lived down in the low desert and as of right now, Jack had guided them up through the winding roads of the mountains into the hi-desert, the mesa in Yucca Valley to be precise.

Kim reached for her cell phone resting in a cup holder in the center console. She wanted to keep it close in case she was forced to make a 911 call to the police. She had no idea of what to expect.

"Damn!" she swore, glancing at the screen. "No service." Frowning, she tossed the phone on the passenger seat. "Oops, sorry. Forgot you were sitting there."

"No problem." Kim could hear Jack's disembodied voice. He was reserving his energy by staying invisible in the earth realm. So he wasn't really sitting there. He was only there in spirit.

Jack projected his voice, telling Kim to take a dirt road that was barely visible, coming up on her right. Over grown tumble weeds and several Joshua trees were blocking her view. Jack explained that she had to take it slow so she wouldn't pass the road up and to keep the car as quiet as possible. If it weren't for his guidance, she wouldn't have been able to see it at all. There was a small abandoned house located at the end of the dirt drive. That's where Ryan had Vienna.

"How much farther down the road?" Kim asked. Being a sports car, the suspension sat pretty low, and the front end of the car was scraping while hitting deep potholes in the grooves of the forgotten, unmaintained road. Dust was kicking up and ballooning into great puffs of brown clouds. She was afraid with all of the commotion their arrival wouldn't be much of a surprise.

"Not far. Park and walk from here," Jack instructed.

"Okay." Kim put the car in park and cut the engine. She left the keys in the ignition for a quick get-a-way. Taking in a deep breath, she gathered her courage before opening the door.

"I'm going to check on Vienna," Jack said. "I'll be right back."

"And leave me alone?" she asked. Even though Kim couldn't see him, she could no longer feel his presence. She knew she was alone.

***

Vienna searched the drawers of the dresser. They were empty. She checked under the bed. There was nothing under there but dust bunnies and rat droppings.

She now doubted that this was Ryan's home. There were no personal belongings in the room. Her fear grew in the pit of her stomach. Where was she?

Reaching over the dresser, she placed her hands on the boarded window. She pushed hard against it, hoping to loosen it. She tried each corner, placing her palms against it and leaning in as hard as she could. No good. The thick board wasn't going anywhere. She was trapped.

A metallic rattling noise got her attention. It was coming from the other side of the door. Vienna froze, standing with her back to the boarded window. What should she do?

The words play dumb came to her. She hurriedly pulled the thick dusty drapes closed over the window and settled back on the bed. Grabbing the ratty pillow, she hugged it close to her chest, tried not to choke on the dust and closed her eyes. Remembering her glasses weren't on when she awoke; she whipped them off and set them on the table.

With a scrape and an elongated squeak, the bedroom door opened. Vienna held still and listened to the slow footsteps growing nearer. Her heart thundered in her ears and she was having difficulty breathing.

A warm hand touched her forehead and swept her bangs to the side, away from her eyes. Vienna fluttered her eyelids as if slowly arousing from a deep sleep.

Ryan's fingertips gently traced her jaw line and stopped at her chin. She could feel his lips brush against hers in a kiss. His breath was warm on her face. It took all her power not to lurch forward, grab hold of him by the throat and squeeze. He had no right to touch her, to kiss her, to violate her. How dare he take advantage of her?

But she listened to her inner voice and stayed still. He was stronger than her. He could easily over power her. She needed to put together a plan.

"Vienna," Ryan hissed into her ear, his lips brushing against the lobe. "Wake up, sleeping beauty. Your prince has arrived."

Vienna fluttered her eyelids again, but this time opened them and blinked hard a few times. Ryan's cold green eyes were focused on hers. She asked, "Ryan? Where am I?"

"Somewhere safe," he answered. He was sitting on the bed next to her, playing with her hair. "You had too much to drink."

"Did I?" Vienna asked, scooting herself back and up into a sitting position. She leaned her back against the wall and protectively drew her legs up to her chest. "I didn't think I had that much."

"I'm telling you, you did."

Vienna looked down at her shoeless feet. "Where are my shoes?"

"Plan on leaving so soon?" Ryan asked.

"Oh, I," Vienna stammered. "I should probably get home. Kim and Bunny will be really worried about me. I should've checked in. What time is it? And where's my phone? I really should give them a call. Let them know where I am."

"Tell me about this dream you've had," Ryan said, getting up from the bed. He walked over to the dresser and stared at the drapes.

"Dream?"

"About Nathan and Sarah," he said his voice low and sinister.

"Oh, that," Vienna's voice softened. "That was nothing. Just a silly dream."

"No," he said, his back still to her. "Tell me."

Even though his voice was low, Vienna knew he was giving her an order. It really freaked her out that his back was turned to her. Maybe it's because she couldn't see his expression. She couldn't see what was going on behind those cold eyes. Were they smiling at her discomfort or were they burning with fury?

She wondered if she should take this chance to try and flee the room. It might be her only opportunity. Too frightened to take it, she tried instead to form words to describe her dream.

"I dreamt this guy met this girl in a red dress at a club then killed her. I, uh, it's just a dream though. Doesn't mean anything. You know, like the dreams people get about being naked at school. Doesn't mean you're really naked at school, does it? I mean, I've had those dreams numerous times and in real life I've never gone to school naked." Vienna knew she was rambling, but it made her feel better. It bought her time. "I even get those dreams where I show up at a class that I forgot to go to all year and I have to take the final. Ugh… those are the worst. Has that ever happened to you?"

Ryan turned to face Vienna. His stern expression was eerie in the candlelight. Sometimes she could make out his features, sometimes times it was all in shadow. "Who was the guy?" he questioned.

"Um, I don't know." Vienna reached for her glasses on the table next to her. She slipped them on.

Nope, he still looks eerie, she thought. Just not as blurry.

"Don't lie to me." Ryan's voice was still low. He took a step closer to the bed.

Vienna's body jerked in response. She pushed her back against the wall. "I'm not."

"Who was the guy?"

"I, uh," Vienna's breathing became ragged, "Nathan, I think."

"How do you know it's Nathan?"

Vienna nervously licked her lips. Her mouth still felt parched, her tongue dry and thick. "I saw him, I mean, in my dream. The girl in the red dress, Sarah, she got up from a table. I think someone put something in her drink, she was stumbling…" Vienna's voice trailed off when she put two and two together. She'd been wrong. Nathan never drugged Sarah. It was Ryan. He did it. Just like he drugged her. She didn't have too much to drink. He slipped something in her glass.

Ryan saw the spark of recognition on Vienna's startled face when she realized the truth.

"You killed her," Vienna whispered. "Not Nathan." She suddenly felt chilled to the bone as if Sarah was now with her in the room, listening.

Ryan grinned, a corner of his upper lip curled up, exposing partial teeth. "I killed them both."

Vienna's body froze. She tried to swallow and couldn't. "But, but why?"

"Sarah was my girl," he said. "We met online in a local chat room, flirted a bit; she was the girl of my dreams. Beautiful, intelligent, and into me. She never even asked to see a picture. She liked me!"

Vienna was afraid to break eye contact with Ryan. She was too frightened to blink.

Ryan chuckled and shook his head. "We scheduled a time to meet. That night at Goldie's I sent her over a special drink. I didn't expect Nathan to tag along after work. The dumb moron ruined my special night."

Vienna gnawed on her bottom lip to keep it from trembling. Ryan's voice was getting louder, more intense.

"Nathan was what you'd call a jock. Not much in here," Ryan said, tapping his temple. "He thought he could have any girl he wanted. And do you know what he did? He saw my Sarah leave the club and chased after her. Stepping in on my girl! He deserved his death," Ryan seethed, his face twisting and contorting into an evil sneer.

Vienna was too afraid to move. She wanted to make a run for the door, but wasn't sure if the timing was right.

"I followed them down the street," Ryan continued. "Nathan was guiding Sarah to his car. I could hear him saying he'd take her home. We came to an alley."

"The dumpster," Vienna whispered.

"Anger boiled beneath my skin. Nathan was stealing my girl. He had his arm around her, walking with her. What would you do? Huh? Tell me? Would you punish him? Has anyone ever taken away your one true love?"

Vienna stared at Ryan. Terrified, she couldn't speak.

"Tell me!" he demanded, raising his voice. "What would you do?"

"I, I don't know," she managed to say, her eyes tearing up.

"I'll tell you what I did. I rammed Nathan from behind!"

Vienna gasped. A tear escaped her eye and rolled down her cheek.

Ryan's voice dropped to barely a whisper, "I didn't…

I didn't mean to hurt Sarah. It was an accident. She hit her head. The blood, the blood was everywhere. I couldn't…" He held out his hands, staring at them as if envisioning the blood.

"She hit her head on the dumpster," Vienna said softly, remembering her vision of Sarah that night in the alley and the horrible headache she had. "I'm so sorry."

"I couldn't save her." He held the palms of his hands up. "The blood… There was so much of it. So red…"

"It wasn't your fault," Vienna sympathized. "You didn't do it on purpose."

"I killed her," Ryan said. "I killed the love of my life. Then I killed him. I grabbed a broken bottle and stabbed him over and over and over while he tried to get up. I kept stabbing him until he stopped moving."

Vienna closed her mouth. She didn't know how to respond.

Ryan balled his hands up into tight fists. His lips tightened into a slim line and his nostrils flared.

"Do you know how heavy this fricken' oaf was? You try dragging a dead body to the car. Let me tell you, stuffing a six foot tall man into a trunk of a foreign piece of crap before rigamortis sets in isn't easy. The only thing this idiot did right was to park his stupid car close enough for me to get him into the fricken' trunk."

"What happened to Sarah?" Vienna asked.

"She died! What the hell do you think happened?" Ryan took another step closer to the bed. His shins were now pushed against the filthy mattress. "Are you judging me?"

"No." Vienna shook her head while trying to think of a way to appease Ryan. She needed to calm his temper.

"None of this was your fault, you know. You did what you had to do. Anyone would understand. Sarah would understand. I know she would. You loved her."

"I buried his body," Ryan continued. "I took him up here in the hi-desert. I buried him in the sand near a grove of Joshua trees. That's when I found this house." He held his hands up in the air and smiled proudly. "Then I drove Nathan's car back to his apartment. I wiped down my fingerprints and parked it on the street."

"Oh," Vienna said. She averted her eyes from his and asked the inevitable. "Why are you telling me this?"

Ryan raised an eyebrow. "You already knew."

"But I didn't," Vienna protested, scooting her back even harder against the wall. "I swear. It was only a dream."

"It's a shame, too," Ryan said. "I felt something between us, a connection. I was going to make you mine tonight. Consummate our new relationship."

Vienna wasn't sure if her eyes were playing tricks on her. A dark shadow, a figure was forming in the corner of the room behind Ryan. She wondered if it was Sarah. Was she really there? The room suddenly became cold. Vienna watched Ryan rub his arms. He, too, was feeling the drop in temperature.

"I feel it, too. There's an attraction between us," Vienna said, stalling for time. "Ryan, it's not too late. We can be together."

Ryan briskly rubbed the palms of his hands together then clasped them tightly in front of him. "But it is," he said. "It's too late for you."

***

"Hurry, now!" Jack's disembodied voice echoed

181

around Kim.

Kim ran up the dirt road approaching the dark house. She stumbled a few times, tripping over rocks, potholes, and sinking in soft spots hidden in the sand. "What am I supposed to do?"

"Distract him," he said. "There's no electricity in the house and the night is too dry. I need energy to manifest."

Kim ran past Ryan's white Ford truck parked in the sandy driveway and up the three steps to the front door.

"Bang on the front door," Jack instructed as he zapped the battery dry from Ryan's truck. "I'll take care of the rest."

"Hello!" Kim screamed while banging on the front door. "Hello!"

Ryan jumped at the sound. "What the…! Who's there?"

Vienna leapt up from the bed. She made a run for the door, but not before Ryan grabbed her arm. She elbowed him, catching him in the chin causing him to back up into the dresser knocking over the candles. He stumbled forward, and Vienna swung at him and missed. Wide-eyed, she froze for a second and gasped as the thick curtains went up in flames.

Ryan lunged at her, catching her knee in his groin. He went down like a sack of potatoes, but not before grabbing hold of her legs as she tried to run, taking her down with him.

Kim leaned her right shoulder into the front door and pushed. It didn't budge. There wasn't a doorknob, only a hole where one used to be. She stuck her fingers through the opening and could feel fabric. Something had been placed in front of the door. With all her strength, she leaned into the door again and again. On the third try, she managed to push it open enough to squeeze inside past an old tattered couch, now a nesting ground for rats.

"Vienna!" she called, entering the dark house. She coughed as smoke began to fill the room. She waved her hands in front of her. "Vienna!"

"Kim!" Vienna screamed. She wrestled on the floor with Ryan. He scooted forward and rolled on top of her, pinning her to the ground with his body weight. His hands clamped down on her throat and tightened. She squirmed against him, but couldn't get free. He whispered in her ear, "You're going to pay for that."

Above them a swirl of dark smoke broke into two and took the shape of hands. A familiar icy coldness slashed through Vienna's body as the black smoky fingers clutched Ryan's shoulders yanking him off of her. It was Sarah.

Vienna scrambled to her feet, escaping the bedroom. She came tearing down the short hallway, gasping for breath. Her throat burned and her lungs ached.

Ryan somehow escaped Sarah's burst of fury. He stumbled out of the bedroom right behind Vienna. He seized her by the hair and yanked.

"Run!" Vienna croaked, when she recognized Kim's figure silhouetted in front of the front door. "Get out of here! Go!"

"No!" Kim screamed, standing still. "Let go of her!"

"Come any closer and I'll kill her," Ryan threatened. "I'll snap her neck. And then you'll be next!"

Ryan jerked Vienna to him. Her head snapped back in response. She could feel his body pushed up against her. The thrill of hurting her was turning him on. He twisted his hand tighter in her hair. His other arm coiled around her waist. Vienna's neck twisted awkwardly at an odd angle. She was afraid her neck would break under the pressure.

"Let go of me you sick bastard!" Her voice was barely audible, but she was sure he could hear her.

"Stay away from her!" Jack's voice thundered all around them. In a glowing display of colors and a flash of brilliant light, he materialized right before their eyes.

Vienna could feel Ryan's body become rigid. His grip on her hair and waist, loosened.

Orange flames licked out around Jack, outlining his now corporeal body with dark shadow. He reached out and grabbed Ryan by the shoulders. "Let go of her!"

Ryan let go.

Without waiting to see what was about to happen, Vienna ran to Kim and together they fled from the house. They ran until they were a good distance down the dirt road. Vienna didn't even feel the rocks or spikes from the goat-head burs penetrating the tender bottoms of her feet as she raced through the desert.

Chapter 15

Vienna was so relieved to be back at her father's house. She sat at the kitchen table and closed her eyes. They were so heavy with exhaustion. She could feel the warmth of the half empty ceramic mug in her hands.

Her thoughts were still reliving the horrors of last night. She was so thankful to Jack for swooping in and saving her life. After she and Kim had escaped Ryan and the burning house, Jack joined them at the rental car. He had used the last of his energy to manipulate a call, even without service, to the police and the fire department using Kim's cell phone.

Vienna and Kim had spent the wee hours of the morning giving their statements to the police of what had happened. Vienna had no explanation as to how Kim found her. But Kim had a set story in mind. It was one that she and Jack had worked out ahead of time. She explained to the police that when Vienna never returned home, she became frantic. She made a phone call to one of Ryan's coworkers, named Chad, who happened to be a guy she knows, who looked up this address for her. The police seemed satisfied enough, even though the house was an abandoned one, and didn't push the question further.

In her mind, Vienna replayed the events of what happened when the police first arrived. She remembered seeing Ryan passed out on the ground where Jack had left him, near a grove of Joshua trees, close to the road.

Somehow Jack had managed to give Ryan a super dose of whatever is was he'd slipped into Vienna's drink at dinner. How Jack got the drugs into Ryan's system was something she wasn't sure she wanted to know. But she bet it was painful.

When the paramedics showed up on scene, they crouched over Ryan's body, checking his vitals and examining him before making the decision to lift him up onto a gurney. Upon lifting him, Vienna's cell phone slipped out of his jacket, falling to the ground. The ambulance driver watching the two paramedics shined his flashlight on the spot where the phone fell.

"Hey! We have something here!" he called to an officer, waving him over. "Something you need to see!"

Ryan's body had brushed the dirt away, exposing two fingers poking up through the sand. Vienna's cell phone lay next to them while miraculously playing back Ryan's confession. Jack had purposely set Ryan down on top of Nathan's shallow grave so that his body would be discovered.

Vienna didn't know for sure, but she believed Sarah had been with her, locked in that scary room, when Ryan confessed. She also believed that it was Sarah who manipulated the cell phone to record the conversation.

"Are you sure you're okay?" Bunny asked. She and

Kim joined Vienna at the kitchen table. The three of them had had a rough night. After giving numerous detailed reports to several different officers, Bunny, took Vienna to the hospital to have her checked from head to toe, but not before she promised to keep this a secret from Vienna's father. Against Bunny's better judgment, she promised that this would be their secret as long as Vienna told her the truth about what really went on that night. Grudgingly, Vienna told her everything, all the way back to the dreams that brought her to the desert to begin with. She left out no details.

"Yeah, I'm okay," Vienna said, leaning her chin on her hand propped up by her elbow. "I could use another cup of coffee."

"Sure." Bunny bounced up from her chair to fetch Vienna a refill. "You deserve another cup after last night."

Kim was frowning into a strawberry yogurt she dug out of the fridge for breakfast. "This is all my fault," she said, dipping her spoon into the cup and stirring. "I shouldn't have talked you into going out with him."

"It's nobody's fault," Vienna said. "How were you supposed to know this would happen?"

"It's not that," Kim explained. "You knew something wasn't right. You kept saying the guy was giving off creepy vibes and I didn't believe you. I pushed you to go out with him. I feel bad."

"Don't. You thought you were helping me get over Brandon. You were being a friend."

"Yeah, a stupid one," she sniffled. "I wasn't listening to you. Next time, just tell me to back the hell off."

Vienna wanted to smile, but couldn't get her cheeks to respond.

"Here you go." Bunny slid a fresh cup of coffee in front of Vienna and retook her seat.

"Thanks. I need to wake up a little before I go."

"Go?" Bunny asked. "Go where?"

"I have something I need to take care of," Vienna said. "Don't worry. I won't be gone long."

Kim put her hand on Vienna's. "Do you want me to come with you? I'll go change real quick."

"No," Vienna said, and took a sip. "This is something I need to do alone."

***

Vienna parked on the street in front of Sarah's mother's house. She stared at it in awe. It was just how she'd pictured it in her mind, a one story ranch house with dark brown stucco and cream colored trim. She believed Sarah was the one that guided her here. It wasn't very far from her father's house, only a few miles away.

"Yes," Mrs. Johnson said, opening the door.

"Hi," Vienna said, and smiled weakly. "You don't know me, but I need to talk to you about your daughter, Sarah."

To Vienna's surprise the woman nodded. Her eyes were misty with tears and dark circles resided beneath them. She led Vienna into the living room and offered her a seat on the couch. She sat across from her on a matching chair.

Vienna explained her story, beginning with the dream and ending with Ryan's confession. The woman nodded. She sniffled and wiped at her wet eyes with the back of her hand.

"Thank you," she said quietly. "I never knew what had happened to my baby girl. Now I know."

"Sarah wants you to know she loves you," Vienna said. "She says she's in your heart." As the words tumbled from her lips she could feel a release of the dark heaviness that had been weighing on her shoulders over the past few weeks. It was as if she could feel Sarah crossing over into the white light of the other side. It was a miraculous, wonderful feeling. Sarah's soul was now at peace.

Mrs. Johnson reached up and played with a silver heart shaped locket dangling from her necklace. "Yes, she's always in my heart," she said, opening the locket to show Vienna the beautiful photos of her daughter inside.

***

After her visit with Sarah's mother, Vienna had one more stop to make before heading back to her father's house and crawling into bed to try to get some much-needed sleep. Something important suddenly came to mind that she needed to take care of.

She knocked on the front door of Goldie's club. Being that it was early in the day, she really didn't think that anybody would be there. But she thought it was worth a try.

After a few seconds, she knocked again and waited. There was still no answer. She turned to leave, deciding to come back later, when the door cracked open behind her.

"Yeah?"

Vienna spun around. It took her a moment before she recognized who'd answered the door.

Goldie was standing there in cut-off denim shorts and a plain white T-shirt with no makeup and no wig. Out of drag, he looked quite different, except of course for the long yellow glittering acrylic nails. Those were still on.

189

Goldie's eyes were bloodshot and swollen like he'd been up crying all night.

"Goldie? Are you all right?"

Goldie swiped at his eyes. "Yeah, I'm fine. This isn't a good time. Come back tonight."

"Wait," Vienna said, before he could close the door. "Your grandma wanted me to tell you something. She says thank you for the flowers."

"My granny?" Goldie swung open the door and quickly ushered her inside. "You saw her? Girl, why didn't you say so? Sit down."

Vienna took a seat at the nearest table. Goldie pulled out a chair next to her. It was just the two of them in the otherwise vacant club.

"It wasn't so much as that," Vienna admitted. "I didn't actually see her. I just had this thought come to me while I was driving and needed to tell you. It felt important." She shrugged. "I'm kind of new at this."

Goldie smiled and nodded. "I put flowers on her grave yesterday. I really miss her. She raised me, you know. My granny was like a mother to me."

"Well, I just needed to tell you that," Vienna said. "I hope you know how much she loves you."

Goldie swiped at his teary eyes again and sniffled. "Thank you. I love her, too."

"Oh, and one other thing," Vienna said. "She wants you to know she's proud of you. And it's okay with her. She wants you to be happy. Does that make sense?"

Goldie nervously clicked his acrylic nails together. "Yeah, it makes sense." He nodded. "Granny was a strict God fearing woman. I was always worried I'd disappoint her. My lifestyle ain't one she'd approve of."

"Don't worry anymore," Vienna reassured. "She understands and is very proud of you. I keep picturing something. I'm not quite sure what it means. I see the color blue. I think she's trying to say she likes the blue one better."

Goldie beamed. "I was trying to decide which dress I was gonna wear. It was between a little blue number I bought recently or my trade mark gold. Thanks, Vienna. I'll go electric blue."

"Don't thank me. Thank your granny."

"Thanks Granny," Goldie said, looking up to the heavens above.

The two of them chatted for a bit. Vienna filled Goldie in on the events of last night then went back to her dad's house for a long, dreamless, well-deserved nap.

Monday, May 2
Chapter 16

Vienna and Kim stayed in Palm Springs through Saturday so she could spend some time with her father. Bunny had been true to her word and kept Vienna's secret from him. Not one word had been mentioned about anything supernatural. Maybe Bunny wasn't so bad after all.

"Tim!" Kim scolded. "Come on now. No paintbrushes in your nose!"

The class giggled, Tim removed the brush wedged in his nostril then went back to work.

Kim turned up the stereo, classical music echoed throughout the classroom.

"So," she said, joining Vienna at the sink. Vienna was washing paint out of used brushes. "Have you heard from Jack?"

Vienna's cheeks reddened. "We've only been back a couple days. Why would you think I've heard from Jack?"

"Let's see," Kim teased, "because he's your spirit guide. And you blushed when I asked."

With her thumb and forefinger, Vienna had rung blue paint from the bristles of a brush. "I'm not blushing," she protested. "And I haven't seen him since, well, you know when…" She kept last night's dream to herself. Kim didn't need to know she'd been fantasizing about Jack. And as of right now, she wasn't too sure if it was just a dream or if it really was Jack. Whatever it was, it was good.

Before going to sleep last night, she'd read out loud a list of guidelines she wrote up. If they were to work together, Jack had to agree to follow them.

The number one rule was no reading her private thoughts. The second rule was no talking in her head, and the last rule was absolutely no jumping into her dreams. She left the list next to her lamp for Jack to read in case he showed up.

After she switched the light off, she laid in bed thinking of Jack, wondering if he was still around. She hadn't seen or felt his energy since that dreaded night with Ryan. Maybe she was being too harsh. Maybe she should let the rules slide from time to time.

Unable to sleep until she wrote down one more important rule, she reached over and grabbed the list from her nightstand. Sliding open the drawer, she snatched a pen and scribbled on the bottom of the paper.

Tonight, I'll make an exception…or until I say otherwise.

"Well," Kim said, bringing Vienna back from her daydreaming. "He's your spirit guide. He's with you whether you know it or not."

"Yeah, I guess so." Vienna shrugged. "I still can't believe that you were able to see him, too. It makes me feel a little less crazy."

Kim grinned. "And he's hot!"

Vienna shook her head and laughed, "You really are something else."

"Chad called me." Kim beamed. "He's pretty cute for a computer nerd. Oh, and I found out that he's only two years younger than me."

"Nothing wrong with that."

"Nah," Kim said with a wave of a hand. "Women live longer anyhow. Dating a younger man makes sense."

"Completely," Vienna teased. "And being that he's a flight away, he can't smother you."

"That's right," Kim agreed. "There's nothing wrong with long distance relationships. They're the best. And it gives me something to look forward to."

"Exactly."

"Oh, and you'll never believe this. I somehow passed my Spanish class. I'm getting a C minus," she said, excitedly. "So, no summer school for me."

"Kim, that's awesome! We'll be graduating together."

"Yup," Kim said. "And since we'll be out of school and have a lot of extra time on our hands, I've been wondering who is next on the list?"

Vienna turned the faucet off and set the brushes on some paper towels to dry. "What do you mean who's next on the list?"

"For us to help?" Kim clarified. "We're a team, you know."

"Yeah, I know." Vienna was very thankful to have Kim for a friend. "We make an awesome team."

Out of nowhere, a girl in the class squealed. Everyone started laughing. This time, Tim, the class clown, accidentally stuck the wrong end of his paintbrush up his nose. And it was loaded with green paint. Green acrylic bubbles blew out of his nostril as he laughed.

"Tim!" Kim shrieked.

Vienna giggled, running to Tim's rescue with a pile of wet paper towels. That's when she felt him. His energy tingled all around her. She knew that Jack was there enjoying the fun, too. In fact, she wouldn't be the least bit surprised if Jack had something to do with the paint brush incident, trying to get her attention.

"I hear you, Jack," she said in her head. "Very funny. And yes, I'm still letting you enter my thoughts… for now."

About the author

Michelle Ann Hollstein resides in Southern California with her two wonderful children and her spoiled kitties. She obtained her degree in Art Studio with a concentration in painting from the California State University of Sacramento and enjoys partaking in creative projects.

She's the author of the quirky and comical Ms. Aggie Underhill Mystery series, the paranormal mystery series, A Vienna Rossie Mystery, as well as the Nonfiction series, Who Says You Can't Paint? She's also the author of the science fiction suspense series, Fatal Reaction, under the name M.A. Hollstein.

You can visit her website at www.MichelleHollstein.com

A Vienna Rossi Paranormal Mystery
Awakened Within
Beautiful Beginnings
Cheating Heart
Ghostly Gig, A Vienna Rossi Halloween Short Story

Ms. Aggie Underhill Mysteries
Deadly Withdrawal
Something's Fishy in Palm Springs
Maid in Heaven
A Hardboiled Murder
One Hell of a Cruise
A Prickly Situation
Vegas or Bust
Dead Ringer
The Case of the Haunted Address
The Mystery of the Beautiful Old Friend
All I Wanted was a Drink
Love is Murder
End of the Rainbow
Coffee, Fireworks and Murder

Nonfiction
Who Says You Can't Paint?
Night Crashes
Joshua Tree
Serenity
Escape

**Books written under the name
M.A. Hollstein
Fatal Reaction**
The Beginning
Survival
Battle of the Hunted
Nightfall

www.ingramcontent.com/pod-product-compliance
Lightning Source LLC
La Vergne TN
LVHW022141300725
817535LV00023B/192